THE SPIDER:
THE SPIDER AND THE FIRE GOD

THE SPIDER AND
THE FIRE GOD

By Grant Stockbridge

POPULAR PUBLICATIONS • 2023

CHAPTER 1
AVATAR OF FLAME

H E CALLED himself Kalki, tenth avatar of Vishnu the All-Powerful. He walked through the streets of New York bare-footed and wearing a white robe that was strange against the fiery fierceness of his red beard and the mane of his hair—and he demanded that mankind desert their churches to follow him. Men laughed, and Kalki lifted his bony scarred hands to the heavens and invoked... *The Fire!*

Afterward, there was no more laughter. Afterward, there were frantic men who bumped their foreheads on the stony pavements and begged insanely for mercy!

For a long while after he arrived in the city, Kalki was patient with the unbelievers for he proclaimed that he had come to restore mankind to purity and virtue, as befitted the tenth avatar of Vishnu. He acquired his scattering of followers and at first the police did not concern themselves with him. That was why, when *The Fire* came, he was too powerfully entrenched to be stopped. He strode, after that, worshiped as a god through cowering streets, and there was only one man to stand between him and the tortured, enslaved people—a man who, himself, was hunted like a wild beast by the police and by the wolves of the underworld... a man who dared not use his own honored name of Richard Wentworth, lest he be slain!

Yet Richard Wentworth was there on the hot summer night

when Kalki vaulted to awful power, when first *The Fire* began to spread its red terror through the city. It was a close night. The sun heat still sulked hostilely in the cavern streets and people crouched on their doorsteps. The voices of the children were muted by the oppression and they moved heavily, half-heartedly about their games. Into these slums, Kalki moved. He walked alone, bare-footed on the blistering pavement, and his fiery, powerful head was bowed.

A few children mocked at him, or hurled insulting filth, but did not disturb his gravity. It was in this way he came presently to where a small group of men and women stood idly listening to hear a street beggar draw sweet music from a violin. A peaceful scene this, where presently death would strike so terribly!

The music of the violin soared and the lean, dexterous fingers of the musician were delicate on the strings—a curious hand for a street beggar. And Kalki ceased his deliberate pacing, lifted his fire-crowned head and stared at the man. Gray-blue eyes, keen and kindly beneath hooded brows, stared back into his and a slight shock ran along the nerves of the avatar of Vishnu. Other men had felt that thrust of mighty will and mind before this, for beneath the guise of the street beggar was the man whom half a nation cursed—and half a nation blessed in their prayers: Richard Wentworth, who was called the Spider....

FOR A moment, the eyes of the two men held and then Wentworth turned back to the street crowd of the people he loved and served. In his music, they gained a momentary respite from the struggle and sordidness of their lives. There, beside a white-haired man, a young girl tilted back her head and sang softly

3

with the violin toward the invisible stars; and the old man wore a smile on his lips. Into their bemusement, the voice of Kalki struck with harsh warning!

"Fools!" he cried. "Worshippers of false gods! I have been patient but... *I have reached the end of my patience!*"

Wentworth turned quietly to gaze on Kalki, and the force of the man reached out and touched him. For the first time, he felt the menace that this powerful figure in its white robes and fiery hair might bring to his city, though as yet he could know of no reason. There was a tautness that crept slowly along Wentworth's nerves. Some hostile, dire thing was here! Kalki was glaring at the people, pumping out roaring words from his deep chest.

"Now!" Kalki cried. "Tonight, you shall fall down on your knees and worship the one true god! You shall abandon your own churches, desert those profane altars. There is no god save my god, and I, Kalki, am his prophet! Down, down on your knees!"

Wentworth could not smile, as his mind told him he should. He took a slow step toward Kalki, tucking his violin beneath his arm... and then he stopped. In the shadows that rimmed the crowd, that pressed in upon it from the hot shelter of the tenement walls, men were moving. He could glimpse them only dimly, but their deft, silent movements were furtive. Instantly, all Wentworth's tautly keyed body was alert.

In appearance, Kalki might be any one of a dozen fakirs come to America to reap the harvest of easy money, but it was strange that he should harangue a street crowd… It was even more odd that he should have for allies such men as those who were ringing in this crowd! A ray of street light picked out one of them—a glowering face beneath a low-pulled hat, and there was an ugly grin on the man's mouth!

"Down on your knees!" Kalki thundered again.

The old man who had smiled at the girl's song was frowning now. He took a slow step forward, his aged hands clenched into fists. His thin old voice was firm.

"You're blaspheming," he said harshly. "I won't stand for it! You've got no right…."

The girl's hands closed on his arm. "Don't, grandfather," she whispered. "He's just some faker or another. Don't, it doesn't mean anything!"

Kalki's eyes burned toward the two through the hot dusk and, behind them, Wentworth saw the shadowy figure of a man creeping closer. Kalki burst out with a furious oath, but it was in a language even Wentworth did not recognize. Kalki lifted his two long-fingered hands and he turned up his face toward the heavens. Wentworth saw that the palms of the man's hands were curiously scarred!

Only for a moment did Wentworth stare at this strange, gaunt man. Then he tucked his violin into its case and, from its recesses, slid into his fist a small-calibered automatic! He dared not carry his usual heavy guns beneath his arms, not while the city seethed with the search for him, but he knew with a sudden fierceness that he would need this weapon tonight. He knew…

He took a step toward the girl and her indignant grandfather…
and the old man suddenly cried out!

Wentworth's narrowed eyes flicked toward the man, saw his
shaking, thin hands lifted like claws before his face. There was a
staring agony in the man's eyes and his mouth warped with sharp
pain. Across his cheeks was the glinting wet tracery of tears and
then… suddenly, *those tears were turned to tiny balls of fire!*

While Wentworth stood rigid, shocked into immobility, by
the utter incredibility of the thing he saw, those streaks of fire
raced upward—little dancing rows of scarlet flame standing out
terribly on the wrinkled face of an old man. He was screaming,
and a gust of flame spurted from his lips, as if the cry itself had
become visible in scarlet against the black breast of the night.

It was in precisely that same moment that the little, dancing
specks of flame reached his eyes. The eyeballs themselves turned
to fire, and spurts of it swept upward. His hair vanished in a
crackling blaze and the man turned and began to run, wildly,
blindly, down the street. His gaunt, long hands, flapping in
the air, were alive with flame and tongues of it jetted out like
serpents' tongues from within his shirt.

After him fled the girl who had been singing and, abruptly,
as she ran, she began to scream with pain. Those two fell close
together upon the pavement, wrapped in a living, seething blan-
ket of consuming flames that danced and romped across their
prostrate bodies—their writhing bodies that were mercifully
stilling at last!

THE THING had happened in a flash of time, in the instant
between the lifting and the setting down of a foot, and the

harsh, booming voice of Kalki still soared toward the hot skies. Wentworth whipped toward him, but another man was before him. This man hurled himself with clenched fists toward the gaunt figure of the avatar of Vishnu with his gauntly

up-flung arms and petitioning face… but the man never reached his side. While his body flew through the air, the flames were upon him. His eyes, and his nostrils gushed with awful flame and he screamed and fell, writhing, upon the pavement. And once more, retreating into the shadows, there was one of those furtive men….

Wentworth's fist-hidden automatic belched in his hand, and he saw the shadowy figure of the man he had spotted stagger in its flight. Wentworth took a long leap toward him before he checked himself. Memory of that other man who had attacked Kalki struck with the force of a blow across his brain. He could not guess by what means this horror of flame was loosed upon human beings. Until he knew, it was best to fight carefully. It was more important to drive away these killers from the remnant of the stricken crowd than to risk imminent fiery death!

"Down, down on your knees!" Kalki was thundering, "and worship the one true god! There is no escape from the fires of heaven, save in the worship of the one true god—and of Kalki, his prophet!"

Men and women fled screaming along the streets and, even as they sought the safety of the encircling darkness, Wentworth saw another, and then another stagger and scream under the hot touch of the fearful flames. He himself crossed the street in two long bounds and pivoted, the gun ready in his fist. The man he had shot lay motionless on the pavement; of the others there was no trace at all… and Kalki's voice thundered on into the close darkness of the night! Presently, there was no one at all to hear him—only Wentworth crouching in the shadows across the street, and on the sidewalk the five torture-twisted figures of the flame-slain people and the man whom Wentworth had shot.

Wentworth's lips were drawn, thin and bloodless, across his sharpened face. He swiveled the gun toward Kalki. The man was silent, bowing his fiery head above his clasped hands and stood that way through a long moment, obviously lost in silent prayer.

They were alone on the street, the prophet of Vishnu and the man who would sell his life cheaply to protect the people whom he served—the man who was known secretly in the dark places of the world as the Spider! He never hesitated to strike down those who preyed upon the innocent, who slaughtered the helpless. And yet, gun ready in his fist, he now hesitated to shoot down Kalki—hesitated while the dead upon whom he had invoked the fire of heaven still lay, black and pitiful before him! Wentworth knew, without aiming, that his gun muzzle was centered on the bowed forehead of Kalki. He had only to squeeze the trigger and the man would pitch to earth amid the bodies of those he had slain. Wentworth had no belief in elemental fire called down from the heavens; miraculous flames had no need of men skulking in the shadows! Then why not shoot? Was it the hypocrisy of that head, bowed in prayer?

Wentworth frowned angrily. Damn it, the man had no way of knowing that retribution was as close to him as the gun in the Spider's hand! Kalki was putting on no act for the benefit of the crowd, for every living soul had fled. Yet… this charlatan *prayed!* WENTWORTH JERKED up the muzzle of his gun and squeezed the trigger. The finger of flame flicked out into the darkness and, on the right temple of Kalki, the fiery hair jerked to the wind of the passing bullet. The man's head lifted. His eyes widened and, in the faint gleam of the corner light, they glimmered as red as a wild beast's!

"That was only a warning!" Wentworth called softly. "The next bullet can kill or maim you! You will order your men to go away. You will come with me!"

Kalki's eyes burned across the darkness to where Wentworth crouched in the shadows. His voice was contemptuous.

"I have no men," he said. "What need of men has the avatar of Vishnu, when the very fires of heaven defend him and do his will?"

Wentworth laughed shortly, feeling anger prickle over his body—anger but also a certain doubt. The sound of his laughter was flat and mocking, ominous. "There is a fire in this gun that will not obey you," he said. "Do as I command!"

Kalki took long deliberate strides toward Wentworth. The white robe fluttered back from the thick columns of his legs and his bare feet made no sound on the hot pavement. His mane of hair was flung back and his head was carried with a proud intolerance. The mockery of the smile upon his solid lips gave place to no words.

Wentworth's eyes were strained narrow with watching, studying the swing of his hands, his every movement—stabbing toward the shadows where had vanished those men who had circled the crowd like hungry wolves. Vanished… Yes, there seemed no doubt that the men had gone and left Kalki here alone. A brief doubt shook Wentworth. In God's name, what could have caused these awful deaths? What purpose could criminals have in such wanton slaughter?

He straightened and his eyes met those of Kalki steadily. He was aware of the intense magnetism of the man. That gaze could be hypnotic to a lesser will; the face had been chiseled with harsh power from an obdurate stone so that all the features were blunt and strongly angular. The eyes were those of a dreamer; wide, liquid and dark despite the anger that burned in their depths. Even in death, this man would know no fear—yet he *must* be made to talk. The secret of this fire, of the killers who struck from the darkness, must be fathomed at once, lest this horror be loosed upon the city.

Wentworth bowed his head with an effect of humbleness, but stiffly for his neck was unused to obeisance. "Thou art Kalki," he acknowledged softly. "Instruct me, master."

The voice of Kalki that had been harsh with anger fell gently now upon the summer night. "It is well," he said. "Thou shalt come with me to the temple."

Wentworth's gun had vanished into a pocket and he clutched the violin case to him with both arms. When he hid his eyes, he seemed utterly what he pretended, a mendicant musician. His patched clothing was clean and a black shoe-string tie set off the soft collar of a worn shirt. He tautened to the faint, searching whine of police sirens.

"The police," he whispered. "This way, through this alley, Kalki. Come with me."

Kalki lifted a broad, powerful hand. "Shall the minister of heaven flee the myrmidons of temporal power?" he asked quietly. "We will wait."

"They will delay your teaching," Wentworth said rapidly. "Will you let pride interfere with your spreading of the word?"

Kalki stood with his broad shoulders drawn back, one of them thrusting free of the robe like a rock shouldering aside the sea. Then he bowed his head, humbly. "I was vainglorious," he said. "I pray pardon. Lead on, man."

WENTWORTH'S FOREHEAD was creased by a knife-edged frown as he led the long-striding Kalki through the alley and by secret ways he must always use in these days of hiding and flight. If this man was a criminal, he differed from all others the Spider had known in a lifetime of fighting the underworld. Yet there was such power in Kalki that Wentworth could not help but believe in his sincerity. If that were so… It was not the first time that criminals had used an honest, a sincere man as a *front!*

"You have disciples at your temple?" Wentworth asked, abruptly.

"A few devout souls," Kalki said.

"Of all races?"

"Of all," Kalki murmured.

Wentworth nodded to his thoughts. Among those, then, he

must seek the men behind this slaughter. Anger flared in him again at the memory of that white-haired man and the attentive girl, consumed in tormenting flame. There was a way by which he could flush the criminals into the open; it would bring the Spider into the very jaws of threatening death, but that was his privilege. If ever this murderous fire were released, the slaughter would be fearful!

"Master," he said, "if I could enter your temple and learn?"

Kalki's fiery head nodded. "Who am I to close the doors against one who comes seeking light?" he asked, humbly.

Wentworth strangled a fierce laughter that rose in his throat. No, Kalki would not close the doors, innocent or guilty! Once Wentworth entered the temple, he would be completely at the mercy of this strange fire that could strike without warning, and without apparent cause… But the killers must come into the open to attack him—and when they did! Wentworth's hand brushed the weight of the automatic in his pocket.

"I have a car nearby, master," he said. "I will drive you to your temple!"

He turned to the side of the alley and, in the shelter of his body, fluttered his hand in a peculiar rhythm before a crevice in the brick wall which emitted a ray of "black light." The doors of a small garage across the width of the alley slid soundlessly open and Wentworth rapidly ushered Kalki into the battered coupé that was parked there. Moments later, Wentworth backed the car clear of the garage, the doors slid shut, and he tooled the lightless coupé toward the street beyond.

His eyes and ears kept keen guard, for after that first faint distant whining, the sirens had been silent—yet the police must be near! Fatal now to be found in the company of Kalki, and with a gun whose barrel would match with the bullet in the body of the man he had slain. Fatal to be arrested in any case, for the police had the fingerprints of Richard Wentworth and they wanted him for murder! The collodion with which he coated his hands always in these days, lest an accidental print betray him, would certainly not help then!

Beside him, Kalki's head was bowed again, his powerful hands clasped before him... They were like that when the coupé rolled almost silently from the mouth of the alley and three pairs of brilliant headlights, converging, slammed into Wentworth's eyes! He heard the shouting challenge of the police, saw a spurt of gun-fire slash high across the night in warning.

"Halt!" a man cried hoarsely. *"Halt, or you are dead men!"*

CHAPTER 2
TEMPLE OF DEATH

WENTWORTH WAS aware that Kalki's head had lifted in fierce challenge and his own eyes swept the street in swift analysis of the trap. Two of the police cars were on his left, one on the right, and in the backwash of the brilliant headlights he could glimpse uniformed men with poised weapons. There was a machine-gun ready to a cop's shoulder! Undoubtedly, the other end of the alley already was blocked. The police must have been even nearer than he had thought to

13

have placed his whereabouts so quickly. These thoughts flicked across his brain while he sought for a way to escape.

Secretly, his right hand moved and slipped the gear into reverse; he kicked a button on the floor and, beneath the hood, an almost silent compressor set to work. Another touch on the button would release a flood of chemical smoke… but he waited. If Kalki's men were nearby, they would interfere now and the Spider might have his chance to strike, to identify the spearhead of this murder conspiracy. He waited… and nothing happened save that the police shouted and tightened their cordon by advancing with their menacing guns.

"*Get out of that car!*" the same voice bawled at Wentworth, and he spotted the man who shouted from the shadows to the right.

Wentworth made his tones frightened, abject. "Sure, sure, we'll get out!" In an undertone, he spoke to Kalki, "Can't you do something? Pull some more of that fire out of the heavens!"

Kalki shook his massive head, "My miracles are to convince the unbelievers," he said in his rumbling, deep voice. "I lift no hand to defend myself." The police were within a score of feet and their guns were as alert as poised snakes.

"*Cut off that motor and get out!*" the order rang again.

The compressor under the hood was laboring against built-up pressure. Wentworth swore softly and kicked the button again, slammed his foot hard on the accelerator and let the clutch pedal jerk out. At his touch, smoke exploded out from beneath the car as the terrific pressure he had built up was released.

In an instant, swirling clouds of impenetrable chemical vapor had blotted out and absorbed the flaring headlights. Under the impetus of sudden acceleration, the car wrenched violently backward into the mouth of the alley. Wentworth's body was bent harshly forward across the wheel. Kalki just caught himself by the swift thrust of his hand against the dashboard and, out in the impenetrable smokescreen, guns went crazy.

Impossible to see the lurid spurt of their powder flame, but the hammer of their explosions filled the night, racketed along the close walls of the alley. Men were shouting out hoarse oaths… Wentworth checked the car as abruptly as it had started, just inside the alley's mouth. He let the motor idle while the compressor still pumped out dense clouds of chemicals. Bullets made a thin whining as they ricocheted from brick walls. He heard the faint, musical tinkle of glass as a headlight shattered, but they were well protected.

Shouts behind him now, and he nodded quietly. Yes, the police were there, as he had anticipated, but he did not think they would open fire, knowing their companions were likely to be hit.

Through a long minute, Wentworth waited while the guns continued to hammer out their medley of death—waited until they began to stammer into silence. The machine-gun cut off its fierce chatter and the shouts were louder by contrast. Wentworth eased the car into gear, and the powerful motor masked beneath the battered hood was scarcely audible. He let the coupé slide forward, cut it sharply to the left on the sidewalk.

A man shouted, and there was a blow on the metal side as he punched himself away from the car. A gun blasted and, even in the haze, Wentworth caught the smoky red of its flame, but the bullet missed an invisible target. The alarm had been given, but still Wentworth held the car's pace to a crawl. His lips were thin, harshly set together, and there was a narrow tension in his eyes. But he could not go fast. He might run down a policeman, and even in this extremity, the Spider would not injure a defender of the law!

Beside him, Kalki spoke quietly, "You have your own miracles, brother. I see that clearly."

The front fender scraped against metal and, dimly, Wentworth caught the flare of headlights. He whipped the wheel over, let the car crawl forward another dozen feet, then stepped hard on the accelerator. The flood of chemicals he had released still flooded the street, but ahead, it was thinning slightly. In an instant, the coupé leaped clear of the swirling cloud. Wisps of vapor seemed still to cling about it, shrouding it in darkness.

Behind, the guns were insane once more, chattering like angry gods. Wentworth whipped around the corner, twisted again at the next intersection and presently flicked on the lights. The reservoir of chemical smoke had exhausted itself. He cut off the compressor and, faint with distance, heard the beginning wail of police sirens.

Out of his eye corners, he was watching Kalki, but the man's huge body, crowding the tight interior of the coupé, was completely relaxed and his eyes, incurious, peered quietly ahead along the dark streets. Wentworth shook his head slightly. The man was an enigma to him. If he were allied with criminals, he

16

must recognize that Wentworth was no peaceful street musician, not with a car ready to hand and equipped with such escape paraphernalia. A criminal might have guessed at Wentworth's identity, would certainly have wanted some information before permitting farther association despite the fact that Wentworth had snatched him from capture by the police.

Kalki continued to stare straight ahead. "My temple," he said, in his muted rumble of a voice, "you will find beside the river on the Eastern piers."

THE WAY to the Temple of Kalki, avatar of Vishnu, lay through the heat-oppressed torpidity of the slums and Wentworth's car rolled swiftly, unswervingly toward the goal. The sirens still whined off to westward like hounds that have lost the scent—and they might pick up the trail again at any moment! It was with half his mind attuned to this problem that Wentworth first beheld the Temple. Afterward he had eyes and thought for nothing else.

A squat, scarlet monster, the temple spread across the eastern terminus of the street and beyond it the black water of the river glinted evilly. Between square-cut columns of black glass, the doors stood open, the only aperture in an otherwise blank facade—a hungry yawning mouth spread to swallow prey. In its black throat, a single spire of pure flame stood straight up. Incredulously, Wentworth realized that this had been a warehouse.

As he stared, a crimson light grew above the flat top of the temple... grew until it became an up-thrusting tower of scarlet flame. Its lurid glare streaked blood across the river water, somberly lit the broad stretch of the street before it. Alongside Wentworth, Kalki began to mutter in a harshly nasal chant. In a strangely accurate cadence with those barbaric words, the tower of flame... *danced*.

Wentworth smothered a curse that leaped to his lips. Impossible that this should be a scene upon the streets of the world's largest city, the capital of the Western world... a scarlet temple where sacred fire danced and a bare-footed priest who could call down devouring fires from heaven!

Wentworth shook himself physically and brought back his mind to reality: those sirens in the distance, and the fact that this man was the ally or dupe of murdering criminals. Fearful menace was implicit in that temple and the "Fire of Heaven," and Richard Wentworth was at the nadir of his strength and power. He drew in a slow breath, trying to think....

A twist of the wheel sent the coupé scudding into the yawning mouth of a dark warehouse's loading door and he cut off the ignition, opened the door. Kalki lifted his head and, for an instant, the red light of the fire brushed across his rugged face, touched the red depths of his eyes. His chant ceased... and the flame was gone. It was as sudden as that.

"Better we walk from here," Wentworth said quietly.

Kalki stepped to the pavement and it was he who led the way, his powerful legs reaching out in long strides. Wentworth followed, his glance stabbing into the shadows about them, but he could detect no trace of watchers... and yet he felt a strange reluctance to enter that temple. He must be doubly cautious in these days when he must walk alone, lest he involve those he loved in affairs which could lead only to their disgrace and death. Formerly, Nita van Sloan, the woman he loved, had known his every secret and was prepared to go on with the battle, carry information to the police if he should fall.

Now, Nita did not even know in what guise he walked, nor where he hid, and it was better so. His path had become too difficult for even the bravery of Nita to follow, though she would have been more than willing had he permitted. But now, gazing toward the maw of the temple, he wished that *she*, at least, knew. He wished that the faithful comrades-at-arms who had fought beside him, and who now watched over Nita, might be here in the background awaiting call.

There was death in this temple, and the threat of death and the knowledge that the gallant turbaned Sikh, Ram Singh, or stalwart Jackson, his chauffeur, was within call, would have helped. It was not that the man who carried the vengeance that was beyond the law—who was known and dreaded throughout the nation as the Spider—could know personal fear. But it was so easy for death to cut short the career of one man. And if he died, who would remain to solve this horror and destroy the killers behind these deathly flames?

SO HE kept watch as he moved forward. There was no movement within the temple but he heard the lifted blending of men's voices in a slow minor chant. It strengthened while they crossed the wide cobbled stretch of South Street. Wentworth was conscious of the irregularity of the stone beneath his feet, of the rasp of his shoe leather and the softer whisper of Kalki's bare soles. The freshness of a stirring breeze from the river fanned his

RICHARD
WENTWORTH ·

cheeks and lifted the oppression of the heat, bringing the odor of rotted pilings. The hoot of a tug was mournful.

Just beside the pillars of opaque glass, Wentworth checked uncontrollably and Kalki turned his head to smile. The expression was curiously gentle on the cragginess of his mouth and jaw.

"There is no danger here… for believers," he said, and strode into the black throat of the temple.

Wentworth wondered, with a wispy smile on his own mouth, if that had been said in warning, but he did not hang back on that account. His violin case was hugged against his chest and the forced stooping of his shoulders made him seem to cringe. He walked with his knees bent. There was no new light but he was abruptly aware that the music had ceased and that men were all about him—men in long silken robes of rich yellow silk.

"I have brought a new brother," Kalki said. "Take him and instruct him."

Then Wentworth felt the thrust of the beady eyes of the yellow-robed priest. His eyes were quick and black as a monkey's, and there was no expression, either of welcome or of hate, on the thousand wrinkles of his countenance. He seemed intolerably old, and the arm that was bared by the draping of the golden silk was a withered stick. His words made a hissing sound in his throat, were mumbled by his tongue, but Wentworth understood that he was to follow. He went through the main hall of the temple.

Here, too, the scarlet and black of the exterior was repeated, columns of black glass against blank walls. Only at the extreme rear of the flat roof, a thread of moonlight crept in. It made a shaft of silver that seemed tangible in the dark and its tip rested exactly on the golden altar where the single spire of flame

burned steadily. Wentworth took these things in while his mind was busily at work. The criminals who worked here must have some secret quarters in or beneath the building.

Where?

It was only suspicion that could link his monitor to that crew, more than Kalki, but it was worth a quick checkup. Beneath his coat, Wentworth's hand moved to a narrow leather girdle about his waist in which a series of tools was nested in vertical pockets and found a small bottle of oil that he had used on stubborn locks during the secret work of the Spider. He loosened the stopper and moved more quickly after his guide as the withered mummy of a man led him rapidly behind the black pillars. He paused, presently, in the blackest shadow of all… and *disappeared!*

FOR AN instant, Wentworth stood stock-still, conscious of the thick beat of his throat pulse, of the dead silence of the temple. Then his straining eyes made out a narrow doorway. He moved toward it softly, went through with an abrupt forward thrust of his body and found the aged priest waiting, his black eyes incurious in the faint gleam of a taper he had lighted. Was there a suspicion of amusement in the multiple wrinkles about the puckered vent of the mouth?

A gesture of the taper indicated another, narrower door and the faint light probed inward to a barren cot and a high, slitted window, tightly closed.

"At sunrise," the priest whispered, "I will come to instruct you!" He held out the taper.

Wentworth accepted the light with a hand that he made

deliberately hesitant and shaken while his eyes covertly probed the man's face. If Kalki was a dupe, could this be the man behind the criminal manifestations of the murderous fire? As if the priest read Wentworth's thoughts, the puckered mouth parted for an instant to show the blackened roots of rotted teeth. It was, perhaps, a smile.

"Many questions," he hissed, "will be answered in the morning."

Wentworth mumbled his answer, humbly, "Sure, sure. Okay. Anything you say."

As he moved toward the entrance of the cell, he tipped the bottle of oil while he moved the taper so that it would blind the old priest. Then he stepped into the cell and was, abruptly, alone.

He heard no departing whisper of feet, but the silence of the temple crept in upon him. Wentworth had to remind himself of the role he played, an ignorant street player convert to a new and strange cult. He let his gaze roam around him experimentally, hesitantly. He mustn't appear too suspicious or let them know he was aware of the tiny peephole up near the ceiling where eyes gazed down upon him. He eased himself to a seat on the side of the hard couch and made swift plans.

He could count on no more than a few hours of delay, perhaps not that much, before the police identified Kalki and came to seek him out. He would be routed out then himself and made a prisoner, if he waited. Leisure would allow him to worm his way into the intricacies of the temple and ferret out the real purpose behind this elaborate camouflage, but there was no leisure... not for him, nor for the people of the city who might so easily fall prey to the monstrous hidden plans of the priests of Vishnu! It might take him weeks or months, supposing he could avoid the police, to get at the secret, and in that time how many hundreds might go the horrible way of those pitiful few human beings whom Kalki had challenged upon the city street!

Wentworth smiled fleetingly. There was another, swifter way. Its danger crossed his mind and he discarded the thought instantly. Abruptly, he was on his feet and he put furtiveness in his every movement. He slipped to the doorway and peered out along the dark hall, listened through a long moment while his eyes scanned the floor. The oil he had spilled showed an iridescent gleam and, as he had hoped, the priest had stepped into it. His trail led plainly off toward the left! Wentworth smiled briefly, then turned and sprang to his violin case and whipped out an automatic, checked its loading while his eyes peered toward the door. And not once did he glance toward the peephole near the ceiling from which watchful eyes surveyed him.

Wentworth reached out and pinched off the taper flame, waited while darkness settled upon him. Yes, it was the dangerous way, but there was a chance he might follow the oil trail; and if the priests knew that he was other than he appeared, wouldn't they be forced to take action against him? Their attack would help to reveal the real culprits and, if he were lucky... he would learn the secret of the Fire!

For an instant, thought froze him in the doorway of his cell. That damnable fire could strike so swiftly, so terribly, and he had no clue to the manner of its use. If they used the fire on him... Wentworth's lips drew straight and thin. It was the risk he must run! He slipped out of the cell and began to feel his soft way along the narrow corridor.

HIS HAND glided along the cool stone of the wall and his feet were soundless on the floor. There was a freshness to the air that went strangely with the thick walls and the waters that washed beneath the building. Wentworth's lips twisted in a curious smile. Air conditioning? It must be so, yet it was a strange accompaniment to the temple of a Hindu god whose name went back beyond the written records of mankind….

His sensitive fingers brushed across the door-less opening of another cell, a third, then his foot found a step that led downward and below him, he could hear the deep rumble of a voice that could belong only to Kalki. A flick of a tiny shielded flashlight showed the oil trail led downward. He moved soundlessly down the steps, and reaching the level of the floor beneath, he paused to listen, to wait.

Those eyes that had spied on him must belong to some inmate of the temple, yet so far he had caught no sound of pursuit, no hint that his deliberately furtive departure from the cell had been observed. Perhaps they were watching him to learn his purpose?

The silence of the temple ate into his nerves and drew them taut. His strained ears began to manufacture sounds to supply the demand of his imagination. He weighed the gun in his fist, shook his head and pressed on. The rumble of Kalki's voice was nearer, but the wall beside which Wentworth crept was unbroken, smooth stone. This must indeed be an ancient wharf, to be built of stone. It could easily date back to revolutionary days and smugglers' activities against the king's tax gatherers. Yes, that was it, undoubtedly. He checked abruptly. Kalki's voice was fading out. He had passed the entrance, yet there had been no break in the wall! There must be some secret door. Wentworth turned back.

Once more he waited, listening keenly, and could detect no hint that he was followed. Carefully, he shielded in his hand the tiny, focused pocket torch and flicked on the beam. Once more, the oily trail of the priest's feet revealed themselves. He had stepped on this block of stone in the pavement… and then there were no more prints! Attentively, Wentworth scanned the corridor wall and his eyes focused on a small rock, darker than the others. It was such a darkness as many hands, resting on that particular block, might cause. With a nod, Wentworth rested a hand upon that stone, stepped in the print of the priest—and a pivot door swung easily open in the wall!

Utter darkness lay beyond, but the voice of Kalki came more clearly, words masked by the muttering rumble of his tones. Wentworth had flicked off the light. But now, experimentally, he allowed a vagrant gleam to stab into the interior, instantly extinguished the torch. His memory had registered the narrow room beyond in that brief moment. It was merely such another corridor as that in which he stood… and Wentworth hesitated. There was no place of concealment in that rock-lined passageway. If he were found there, he could offer no explanation that would suffice for it was within the secret barrier of the door. Too, he would be in a cell from which escape would be difficult, if not impossible. Yet the oily trail led straight on.

Wentworth deliberately pocketed his torch and took a fresh

grip on his automatic. He stepped through the secret doorway and leaned his shoulder against it to swing the portal shut. It would not move. Wentworth swore under his breath, put more strength into the thrust—and heard a whispered sound! It was no more than the dry rustle of something against the stone but to Wentworth's keen brain it meant that he was followed. That was the whisper of a priest's silken robe. Wentworth pivoted, backed slowly away from the doorway with the gun ready in his fist.

Abruptly, light slashed into his eyes, blindingly. With dazzled vision, he saw a yellow-robed priest surging toward him—a face twisted by rage and murder-lust. Wentworth checked, lifting his gun, and his foot slipped on the oil-smeared floor. As he went down, he caught the exultant hiss of the priest's whispered curse. He saw the glittering, foot-long blade of a razor-sharp knife strike straight down toward his throat!

CHAPTER 3
PRIEST OF VISHNU

IT SEEMED to Wentworth that his brain never worked more swiftly than in the fatal press of battle, when death hovered close above him and he knew that life hung by a hair. Two thoughts, and their instantaneous conclusion, flashed across his mind in the moment while he plunged toward the floor with that villainous knife reaching for his throat. The priest had attacked with the utmost silence, as if he too wished to escape arousing the other priests of Vishnu. Also, the man used the knife like a westerner, chopping downward, instead of using the murderous upward rip which the East has perfected—yet in his facial cast and general makeup, the man seemed an Oriental. This, then, was one of the criminal band!

Wentworth knew those things without conscious thought, even while he mustered his strength for the death struggle. And it was because of that instant analysis that he did not fire his automatic. He pointed his weapon upward and, with a quick twist of his wrist, parried the powerful downstroke of the knife so that it glided past within a fraction of an inch of his throat.

The next moment, the man's body slammed heavily down upon Wentworth's chest, and Wentworth's left hand, light and swift as a sword-thrust, found and prodded violently into certain nerves in the man's throat. There was a convulsive jerk, a stiffening of the body that pinned him down and, afterward the priest went limp. The man's left hand relaxed from the flashlight he carried and it made a faint metallic clatter on the stone floor.

The broad beam flung their single conjoined shadow upon the wall, a grotesque thing of multiple limbs, until Wentworth found and freed the switch. He rolled the priest gently to the floor and lifted to his feet. His breath came easily and deeply through his nostrils and he listened with painful attention. Kalki's voice rumbled on....

In the darkness, Wentworth allowed a swift smile to cross his lips. It was not Kalki that he wanted. The silent ferocity of this man's attack was the strongest proof that Kalki knew nothing of the secrets Wentworth wished to penetrate. He bent and, in the darkness still, found the knife and thrust it through his belt, pocketed the flashlight. Deft movements rid him of his coat and, a few heartbeats later, he settled the priest's golden robe over his shoulders. His plans were already laid.

He worked his own coat upon the unconscious priest, heaved the limp body to his shoulders and left the narrow corridor by way of the secret door. Foot and hand pressing the stones thrust it back into place easily from outside, and he turned toward the stairway that led upward. To anyone who saw him now, he was merely a priest with a prisoner. It was possible he could reach the street; barely possible....

Wentworth took the stairway with swift, lithe strides. Once away from the temple, he could question this man at his leisure and attempt to wrest his secret from him. There were cold depths in his gray-blue eyes. For those who loosed the fearful Fire upon humanity, there could be no pity—not in the Spider's heart! He thought that he might succeed in making the man talk!

He was in the corridor now that led past the doorless entrances to the cells. That which had been assigned to him was near the exit into the temple itself, which he could dimly see—a dimmer gray against the blackness of stone walls. It was the flicker of the altar flame which gave that hint of illumination. Wentworth moved silently toward the exit... and then, faintly, an alarm tingled along his nerves.

He could not be sure at first that he actually had heard anything. These thick walls muted all sounds within and without the temple, but the rumor of a noise came again. In the same instant, he identified it. A bare-footed man was running on stone, the thud of his heels more a vibration than an actual sound. Wentworth swore. The man was in the central hall of the temple… and the noise grew more distinct. He was running directly toward the darkness where Wentworth crouched!

WENTWORTH HURLED himself with great, leaping bounds toward the doorway of his own cell! His toes, the flapping of his silken robe, lifted a whisper through the close corridor that blotted out the thud of running feet, but he knew without question that it would be very close.

The doorway was only scant feet away when he caught the flicker of movement against the grayness of the temple entrance. With a fierce bound, he reached the cell, struck his shoulder softly against the stone-faced arch and caromed into the cell itself. He reeled, off balance, thudded down gently on the couch and was glad that it was stone and soundless. In the corridor, the thud of running bare feet was distinct now.

"Awake, brothers!" the priest cried. "Awake! The police have come for the master!"

A fierce oath sprang to Wentworth's lips, but he checked it. His plan was ruined before he could more than start to put it into execution. Not the remotest chance of escaping now with his prisoner. Swiftly, Wentworth sprang to his feet. His robe was of a different type than that worn by Kalki and the mummy priest, for it covered his shoulders and voluminous sleeves stretched to his wrists. He nodded in approval while he stooped to strip off his shoes and socks and hurriedly worked them onto the limp feet of his prisoner. He stooped then over the unconscious figure, made a deftly expert search of his pockets in the darkness.

Outside the cell, there was the rapid, frantic patter of bare feet, and a voice burst in at the doorway. "Out, brother! The police have come for the Master!"

"I'm coming," Wentworth mumbled. "Coming, right away."

He straightened, thrusting the contents of the other man's pockets, still unexamined, into his own. There was time for no more. He stooped again to make certain, by a new thrust at the throat nerves, that the man would remain unconscious, and then he joined the rapid shuffle of priests in the corridor. Lights were brighter now in the temple and, ahead of him, a robed man lifted his head and began a slow, rhythmic chant.

Pacing to its cadence, the men moved passively forward, hands thrust into their sleeves, heads bowed so that their voices came out, muffled and thick. It almost seemed that one great, rumbling voice poured out the minor melody of the chant. Wentworth was one with them, bare feet shuffling in their traces, head bowed humbly. It might be that he was merely exchanging one peril for a greater one. He was surrounded by enemies who, the moment they glanced toward him, must realize that he was masquerading. But if the police identified him as the man who had helped Kalki to escape, if they took his fingerprints....

The priests were filing out now into the temple and Wentworth, under lowered brows, glanced swiftly about. The flame leaped higher on the altar. He realized, dazedly, that hours must have passed during his taut search of the temple for, where moonlight had thrown its silver shaft across the great hall, there was now a beam of sunlight. Wentworth saw that the break in the roof was exactly calculated to bring the first ray of the sun to the altar… Kalki was blending sun mysticism with the worship of Vishnu.

He had only a fragmentary glance for this fact, for the other files of priests were issuing from three other doorways. He stared toward the main entrance of the temple. Dwarfed there by the high, glittering lift of the black glass columns, was a group of men… an even dozen of them. Ten wore police uniforms and gripped guns in their fists and, of the two in plain clothes, Wentworth identified one at once. There was no mistaking that straddled stance, the military curtness with which he lifted his close-cropped head. It was the acting commissioner of police, Sanford Dane!

They seemed as out of place among these chanting priests— as if they were invaders from another world; another age. The chant of the priests worked their old magic. Hard to realize that outside this building was New York City with its slums and swift subways and the thousand appurtenances of modern western civilization.

Wentworth knew a sudden swift fear; not for himself. He was accustomed to the hourly peril of his life, though he knew abruptly that the men about him already had made their discovery that he was a stranger and no part of their ranks.

They were closing in upon him and, under lowered brows, he caught the swift, inimical thrust of black eyes. There by the altar stood the mummified figure of the old priest, his bald head intercepting the first red ray of the sun.

WENTWORTH SAW Sanford Dane jerk his head and one of the policemen fired a shot upward toward the roof. The crash of the weapon was puny in the immensity of the temple, but its effect on the priests was instantaneous. Their chant broke into harsh cries of rage and, with a swirl of gaudy silken robes, they were racing toward the tiny group of armed men, picked out against the red glow of the sun that was bathing the street behind them. The police guns lifted, centered. Sanford Dane stepped forward with an upthrown hand, and his deep voice bellowed.

"Stop this mummery!" he shouted. "Bring out this fellow who calls himself Kalki or we'll take the place apart!"

Wentworth had deliberately hurled himself forward with the others and he was a bare fifty feet away from Dane when the challenge was hurled. This was madness, or insane courage, he did not know which. The guns of the police could wreak fearful damage here, but against these fanatics they would accomplish nothing. And there was always… the Fire!

These thoughts raced through Wentworth's brain while he kept a keen eye on the men about him. One of them might well take advantage of this scramble to slip a knife into him… for the sake of safety. The priests rushed on, unchecked. Dane stepped back and lifted a hand in signal to the policemen.

Wentworth caught a fragmentary phrase… "Over their heads!"

The guns crashed and the spurting flame of the revolvers

With harsh cries of rage, the fanatics were charging the tiny group of armed men!

seemed to reach out and touch the front line of priests upon their foreheads. The line swayed back, momentarily checked. A throwing knife slashed across the morning redness and a policeman staggered back with the hilt jutting from his shoulder. Death, and the promise of death, was thick and treacherous in the air.

Dane's bulldog face was flushed, red with anger. He lifted his hand in a signal that Wentworth knew would send hot lead thudding into the bodies of the priests and then… Kalki spoke!

Kalki's voice thundered from the remote depths of the temple, but it rang clearly and the words beat upon priests and police with a studied cold contempt.

"Fools, do you think to invade the temple of Vishnu with your puny weapons? Begone, before the fires of heaven wipe out your blasphemy!"

The priests swayed to a halt. They looked about them, as if awakened from a madness, but there was still fierce anger in their eyes.

"Back!" Wentworth sent his whisper among them. "Back to the altar. The Master can handle these fools!"

The nearest men turned their hostile dark eyes upon him, but others beyond did not know who had spoken and their fierceness abated.

"Kalki!" the name poured from many lips like a prayer. *"Kalki! Avatar of Vishnu! In thee, our strength!"*

Wentworth tensed.

The files of priests reformed and presented a banked, solid rank of defenders about the altar. It was only then that Wentworth could see Kalki. He stood on a raised eminence, fronted by a broad, high ramp of steps, at the extreme rear of the temple. As the priests reformed, he came forward slowly, and Wentworth had a flashing memory of folklore in which great men walked heavily upon the earth—walked so heavily that each step sunk them ankle deep in the stone. Kalki's impressiveness was like that. The sunlight seemed to center in his proud, fiery head.

"Begone, fools!" he called again. "Kalki has spoken!"

Sanford Dane took a choppy stride forward. "Sergeant," he

ordered sharply. "Take two men and arrest this charlatan on a charge of murder!"

WENTWORTH ALLOWED a slight smile to touch his lips, though fear for the police leaped high in his breast. He could not help thinking how differently his friend, Stanley Kirkpatrick, would have handled this situation.

Kirkpatrick still held the appointment of police commissioner but for the present it was little more than an honorary title. A serious heart attack had invalided him from office. There was hope that he would regain his old strength, but for the present Dane handled—or rather mishandled, as Wentworth saw it—the leadership of the city's police force. For now he ordered his men forward into what was plainly grave danger. Kirkpatrick would have led the way himself! Perhaps the police felt the fault in Dane, for the sergeant's step lacked crispness as he moved forward—with a gesture drawing two uniformed men behind him.

The sergeant rolled his shoulders forward with an aggressiveness that he had drilled into himself through long hours on the beat. But Wentworth saw that, secretly, he made the sign of the cross! Evidently, Kalki saw it, too, for his voice boomed out angrily.

"Stop!" he commanded. "Bring none of your blasphemies into the temple of Vishnu! You infidel! You worshipper of false gods!"

Wentworth saw the sergeant's Irish jaw set as solidly as rock. "Infidel, is it?" his mutter came softly. "Well, we'll be seeing how you like the feel of an infidel nightstick!"

His stride lengthened, the two uniformed men pressed close

37

behind him. Kalki waited, his leonine head pulled forward, his poise quiet. Abruptly, he tilted back his head, his long, scarred hands lifted… and a cry of horror pressed to Wentworth's lips! It was the gesture with which Kalki had called down the destroying flames!

Even as Wentworth started forward, two priests closed in upon him and he felt the prick of long keen knives reaching through his silken robe. A great, hoarse cry burst from the sergeant's lips, and from the floor before him sudden towering flames leaped high into the air!

Wentworth relaxed with the realization that the fire, for the moment at least, would not be turned upon the police. His eyes narrowed as he studied the curtain of flame that shimmered and danced half the height of the temple's ceiling.

Kalki was plainly visible through the scarlet and gold of the fire, his hands still uplifted. The sergeant tried to stand his ground, but he was alone; the two patrolmen had fled with broken shouts of terror at the upward surge of those sudden flames—and the heat was driving the sergeant backward. There was a black scorching of the stones above which the flames danced, but Wentworth could descry no source of fuel, no reason for that fire… no *natural* reason.

He felt anger surge up through his veins and knew that it was an acknowledgment of unconscious fear. It rode the small squad of the police hard, and Sanford Dane's shouts were drowned in the rising, triumphant chant of the priests. They began to march in a slow, weaving pattern about the altar—and the knives goaded Wentworth to follow.

He glanced at his captors from his eye-corners and knew that his death was written. So
soon as they had him for a moment out of the
sight of the police, those knives would drive
in through his kidneys—and sudden, painful
death would crush in upon his soul!

Under that fearful menace, Wentworth
nevertheless drove his mind to an entirely
different problem. He realized now that it was
imperative that Kalki be arrested. It did not matter whether,
actually, he was party to the criminal conspiracy that burgeoned
here. He was the spear-point of the resistance; the standard
bearer for the priests. If he were placed under arrest, then the
real leader of the criminals must come forward.

Hands still folded inside his sleeves, Wentworth let his fingers
play over the contents of the leather girdle about his waist and
a secret smile touched his lips. Occasionally, he had need of
explosives and he carried, in two vials there, fluids which, when
kept separately, were harmless, but blended together they were
more powerful than trinitrotoluene.

He slid out a small capsule and with skillful fingers spilled
a little fluid from each vial into the halves, pressed the capsule
carefully together again. His eyes flicked over the assemblage.
SANFORD DANE was shouting himself red in the face,
trying to drive his men forward to the attack. The priests, ignor-
ing them, went on with their triumphant chant and, behind his
veil of flame, Kalki waited, arms folded, his massive face calm.
Staring at him, Wentworth knew once more the touch of dread.

Regardless of his methods, the man had the power of instant horrible death at his fingertips. If once he loosed that on the police....

The knives goaded him sharply. There was a warm tracery of blood upon his body. He could feel it beneath his clothing and there was no mercy in the hard black eyes of the two priests beside him. They were compelling him toward the high altar, and Wentworth sensed, from the tension in their faces, that the moment of his death was close at hand.

He thought he gauged their plan. Behind the altar, where his own file of priests would pass in a moment, he would be out of sight of the police. Obviously, they feared he might interfere— might in some way betray them. It was just there, behind the altar, that the knives would strike home! Wentworth's jaw set rigidly, and his hand clenched about the capsule of explosive. He had concocted only a light mixture that would produce a minor detonation, useless against these men. His eyes glanced swiftly toward the altar, and the spire of flame at its crest. He was almost abreast of the pinnacle of golden stone.

What he had to do must be done with absolutely no preliminary tautening of muscles to warn the two priests. It would call for the utmost coordination of his perfectly trained body and split-second precision of timing. He slid his hands almost free of his sleeves and waited until he felt the knives drawn back minutely from his flesh. That would be the moment when they tensed their muscles to drive the blades home, to snuff out the Spider's life! He thought they would act together. If they did not....

Wentworth felt the hard tension of his jaw muscles; there was an unavoidable bounce in his step that came from the tautening of all his thews… the body's reflex protest against death. He was abreast of the altar, passing it slowly, turning behind it. When he was completely hidden his acutely attuned senses ached with the force of concentration. Had those knives relaxed a fraction? He must wait, *must. Now!*

Wentworth's left arm swung backward without preliminary tensing, and swung with the swift, sureness of a death blow. At the same instant, he pivoted away from the right-hand knife. His tensed left fist caught the knife wrist of the priest on his left. He felt the burn of the other priest's knife sliding across his ribs, missing by the merest fraction of an inch. No time to fight with these two men. With that whirl to the left, he hurled his body violently forward. His right arm arched upward and from his fist flew the tiny capsule of explosive… straight toward the altar flame!

It exploded, tremendously, and the flame leaped high above the altar… was gone… the sacred altar fire extinguished. Even while the stunned, despairing wail of the priests soared toward the vault, Wentworth leaped away from the murderers. With a fury of effort that strained his lips away from his teeth, that drove him in yards-long bound's across the temple floor, the Spider hurled himself violently… straight at the impassive giant figure of Kalki, avatar of Vishnu!

CHAPTER 4
AVATAR OF DEATH!

WENTWORTH WAS acutely conscious of every-thing that went on about him, of the hiss and crackle of the fire curtain which Kalki had called into being; of the wails of the priests over the extinguished altar fire. Through all that, too, he could hear the hoarse orders of Sanford Dane, felt the anger of his tones.

Kalki was resplendent in the lurid light of the flames. His white robe was silken, and red shadows of illumination chased themselves across it, burnished the dark smoothness of his bared shoulder, haloed in his hair. Kalki turned a slow, puzzled face toward Wentworth.

There was time, while Wentworth's feet thrust against the stone floor hurling him toward the avatar, for him to glimpse the mounting reddish gleam in the man's eyes, for him to watch incredulity, then anger, leap into the blunt features. Kalki lifted a condemning hand high into the air, his lips parted from the strong square of his teeth. And Wentworth knew that in the next instant, Kalki would pronounce the words which seemed to draw the consuming flames from the air itself!

To Wentworth, the long reaching of his legs seemed to accomplish nothing. He could hear the silken flutter of his golden silken robe, the rasping expulsion of his own breath. There was even the blurred coldness of the stone beneath his feet, though they were numbing under the pound of his sprint.

Sharp thuds behind him—that would be the feet of the murderous priests he had eluded.

Something hissed past his ear and, out of his eye corner, he caught the flickering gleam of a thrown knife that had just missed him. It angled off into the darkness of the rearmost reaches of the temple and rang on the stones with a silvery, long-drawn note. Two more strides... and Wentworth hurled himself through the air at Kalki!

He saw the welts of muscles rise on the man's shoulder and cord his bare legs as he braced himself for the attack; saw the beam-like arms reach out and the long fingers set for his throat. But Wentworth had no intention of matching physical strength with the thews of Kalki. There was not time, and he could not afford to have the issue in doubt.

He ducked under those out-reaching arms and, as he dodged past, his left fist drove with all his strength and momentum into the pit of the giant's stomach. The jar that struck his shoulder was as numbing as a bullet shock, but Kalki wavered, bent painfully at the waist and Wentworth struck again. He pivoted on his heel just beside the giant, while those great arms arched about to grip him, and his right fist hammered home beneath the man's ear. Kalki's knees went lax. As he pitched toward the floor, Wentworth's shoulders rocked with the drum-roll rhythm of repeated blows.

The shouts of the priests were like the screams of bereaved women. Their golden pattern about the altar was disrupted and became a wave that rolled toward the fallen Kalki—toward

Wentworth where he stood, momentarily stilled, above the powerful body of the leader.

Wentworth saw a knife-arm whip back for a throw and he bent double as he whirled in flight. He had a sudden sense of dimness in this vast temple and realized that the curtain of flame had subsided, punched out apparently by his hammer blows that had blotted out the senses of Kalki. The shouts of the police lifted in a triumphant roar and their shod feet rapped out a sharp, running charge.

There could be no hesitancy in Wentworth's flight. His pause beside the body of Kalki had lasted for no more than a heart-beat. Now his powerful thighs hurled him toward the obscurity that lurked behind the black glass columns of the temple. Behind the fifth from the rear was the door that led to the cells. If he could reach that and resume the role of the aged musician who had befriended and been accepted by Kalki….

A knife rang off the glass column as Wentworth whipped around it. Two strides and he lunged through the doorway, caromed through the entrance to his cell. His hands already were ripping the silken robe from his body and he glanced toward the priest he had laid, unconscious, upon his cot. An oath leaped tearingly to Wentworth's lips. For him, there could be no safety in the role of the aged musician. The man whom he had dressed in his own clothing lay prone upon the cot as Wentworth had left him, but there was this difference. Between his shoulders jutted the hilt of a knife!

NO MATTER. He could not delay. In quick, heaving movements that strained even his whipcord muscles, Wentworth

jerked up the body and drew the robe down over the man's head, then flung himself prone beneath the cot.

The next instant, a yellow-robed priest slammed in through the door, a knife drawn for the death thrust! He stared in bewilderment at the corpse upon the couch, took slow strides forward. His bare feet were within an inch of Wentworth's hand and, violently, Wentworth stifled his laboring breath.

He was aware now of the sticky moisture beneath the cot, seeping in through his shirt. There was the smart of the knife scratches upon his body, and the hammer-hammer of his heart. The odor of blood was sickeningly sweet in his nostrils. More priests jerked to a halt in the hallway just outside the cell and Wentworth was glad that the man stood over him, to deepen the shadows beneath the cot. He could hear the man's harsh breathing; his feet moved with a small whisper on the stone.

"Our brother... murdered!" the man rasped, then he whirled and his voice soared. "After him. He cannot be far ahead!"

His bare foot slipped a little on the stone. He stumbled, caught himself on the wall and then was gone; the doorway was empty.

Beneath the cot, Wentworth sucked in a slow, shuddering breath. Fatal to remain here. He rolled out, started for the door... then turned. There was a thinning pressure in his lips. They would learn presently that one of their own number had killed this priest and, when they did, it was well that they should know with whom they fought! Well, that they should know who had slipped into their fold and claimed a life!

Wentworth's hand slipped inside his shirt to the leather girdle, and a thin, platinum cigarette case glinted in his hand. He thumbed open the base and, on the stone wall above the cot, he pressed the bottom of the lighter. Then he whirled to the door, and ducked into the darkness that still resounded to the shouts of the priests and the furor of the police in the temple.

Behind, on the wall he left a gleaming signature in vermilion, traced as if in blood, a thing of hairy, tensed legs and poison fangs—*the seal of the Spider!*

He heard the quick shuffle of bare feet upon stone and twisted into the doorway of another cell. Three priests bolted past an instant later and their hurried voices called ahead. "Come, come! The police take the Master!"

Wentworth smiled thinly. This was the interruption on which he had counted, should it be necessary for him to make his escape. He waited, motionless, until the rush of priests, the whisper of bare feet and the fluttering rustle of silken robes, went past him, then he slipped out once more and hurried toward the stairway that led downward. No need of light for him. Once his eyes had glimpsed a scene, it lay perfect in his memory.

Long jumps took him down the steps and he checked to lay hand and foot upon the stones which would open the secret room. The door pivoted under his thrust and he leaped through, left it standing open. Let the police penetrate the innermost secrets of this temple! Perhaps it would lay a burden of difficulty upon the future operations of the murderous sect!

ALONG THIS unknown corridor, Wentworth made his way more carefully. He found here a replica of his own cell on a larger scale. The golden shrines of Vishnu upon the wall marked it for the quarters of Kalki himself.

Here, too, was a small altar on which flame burned, throwing its clear light upon the shrines, which pictured the nine previous incarnations of Vishnu, known as the Preserver in the Brahman triad of gods. Wentworth thought bitterly, while he studied the shrines, that Kalki—as he called himself—had taken on more of the characteristics of Siva, the Destroyer!

Here were the representations of Matsya, the Fish, which was the first incarnation, or descent, of Vishnu from the heavens of the Hindu gods—which Vishnu was supposed to have assumed to preserve Manu, the first ancestor of the human race, during the universal deluge. There was the descent, or avatar of the Tortoise, assumed by Vishnu to support the earth when the gods were churning the sea for the beverage of immortality, Amrita; of Krishna, the invincible warrior, who by his exploits relieved the earth of tyrants, and so on to the tenth avatar. And there, mockingly, was a golden image of the man who called himself Kalki! Kalki, Wentworth knew, was the traditional Brahman name for the tenth and ultimate avatar of Vishnu—the descent in which the "Great Preserver" would put an end to all vice and wickedness and restore the race of mankind to purity and virtue!

Jarring laughter forced itself between the set lips of Richard Wentworth. So this Kalki had come to lead the world to purity and virtue—by way of murder! The cigarette lighter was still in his fist. It was something stronger than himself that drew him across the room, which lifted the lighter to implant beneath that mockery of religious faith, the menacing seal of the Spider's vengeance.

Now....

He pressed the seal upon the stone, stepped back to glare at the shrines, then whirled to set about the search of this apartment which was the thing for which he had come. Perhaps, here at last, he could find some clue to the method by which this false prophet brought forth his hell fires. Perhaps, here....

A harsh voice thrust at Wentworth from the doorway of the cell. Wentworth's head jerked up to stare into the black eye of a revolver muzzle, to peer beyond it into the savagely angry face of... Sanford Dane, Commissioner of Police.

· KALKI ·

"Lift them," Dane snarled. "Lift them high, Spider! By God, this time, I've got you dead to rights!"

Wentworth's eyes seemingly did not waver from a steady regard of the small, hostile orbs of the police commissioner, yet the whole scene was registered clearly on his retinas. Dane was alone—at least no other police were visible behind him. But the man was a splendid shot and he stood a full ten feet away... too far for a leap.

Wentworth knew a fleeting gratefulness for the fact that his face and appearance were disguised; at least he could not be readily identified as Richard Wentworth. But that was a small thing. His fingerprints would betray him to the police, and that mocking seal on the wall behind him would send him to the electric chair! Too many times, the Spider had flashed ahead of the police, to strike down the criminals they could not reach by legal means. Justice, without a doubt; a boon to mankind, certainly... but in the eyes of the law, a boastful murderer! How could the Spider be anything else?

SANFORD DANE was already lifting his heavy voice, calling to his men to come and take the Spider prisoner. There was fierce exultation in his tone, a complete readiness to kill in his eyes. No, he would not hesitate. Let Wentworth so much as move a finger, and five leaden slugs would pound into his unprotected body in a space of heartbeats... the dying heart-beats of the Spider!

Dane was a squat colossus across the only exit to the cell, and too far away to reach. Wentworth's hands lifted slowly, and he forced relaxation over his body, assumed an almost lounging posture.

"Why, yes, Dane," he said equitably, in a harsh, disguised voice, "it would appear that you speak the literal truth, for once. You have me dead to rights."

There was no relaxation in the broad-shouldered tense figure

narrow, terribly narrow. Perhaps two inches! Could he drop and balance himself against the smooth front of the building? But he had to! A swift plan formed in his mind.

HE DROPPED, and his toes clutched at the ledge, but he made no attempt to hold his balance. He threw himself sideways, his hands clawed the ledge and he let his legs swing over into space—swing downward toward the other glass column. There was scant chance that his fingers would have the strength to hold if he had miscalculated. No chance at all, but… His scrambling legs hooked about the column, the grip of his fingers on the capital projection was torn loose, and he was shooting toward the pavement forty feet below!

Wentworth clamped his legs as tightly as possible about the column and the cloth began to bind, to slow him a little. His arms reached and he strained his chest against the glass-smooth surface. Below him, he heard a startled shout and knew that his descent had been spotted. Brief fractions of a second later, the cry was echoed from above, but Wentworth could give no heed.

All his attention was concentrated on exerting the utmost of his strength to slow his descent down the glass pillar, so that he would strike with less than stunning, crippling force. He twisted his head about to peer downward. Crowds, prison van, police, swam up toward him at dizzying speed. The cops were drawing their guns, but they held their fire. They crowded in about the bottom of the column, ready to seize him. Wentworth's lips could still part in a smile of mockery. Fools!

There was a definite checking of his speed, though the flesh of his thighs and arms was numbing, burning under the pres-

sure. His shirt was shredded from his chest. Wentworth knew
now that he could manage the drop without serious injury—if
he could utilize the tumbling skill which he had perfected as

The flames were following the prison van, even as Kalki had threatened!

part of the ruthless training to which he had subjected his body for these battles against knaves.

Twenty feet above the ground, he clamped down more strenuously with his arms, shut his teeth on the pain of the friction-scorched skin and... freed his legs. When they swung straight down, he was within ten feet of the ground and he released his arm hold also. There was a concerted, muffled shout from the police, attempting to scatter from his path. Too late...

Wentworth's feet struck the earth, and he used his sprung legs as a cushion, threw his weight backward in a rolling somersault!

The shock of the landing numbed his legs, sent jarring pain through his spine... but the police had not been able to get clear. Wentworth's backward roll hurled him against the chest of one of the men and they hammered together to the earth. Wentworth completed his somersault, came dizzily to his numb feet... and was running wildly across the barren stretch of South Street! The cop lay where he had been hurled, out cold!

Instantly, the confused shouts of pursuit rang out. Wentworth cut across in front of the waiting prison van and wavered in a crazy zig-zag flight. He did not fear the guns from the roof so much. Unless the police there were extraordinarily skillful shots, they would miscalculate in firing down from a height and their bullets would fly over his head. One of the cops behind him was out cold; but the other two... Their guns began to thunder.

Wentworth's feet were numb with pain, with shock, and the cobbles were rough. He tried, fumblingly, to pick the spots where they would hit. His stumbling course had one advantage. It made precise aim by the police doubly difficult. Wentworth lifted his eyes toward where his car was parked, pointed toward the temple. Not a chance. He would have to circle, come back to it....

A FIERCE shock struck his left thigh, twisted him in his flight and hurled him, pin-wheeling, to the cobbles. He rolled, lay motionless on his face and bitter hopelessness twisted his firm mouth awry. There was only shock now, but pain would come swiftly... if the bone were not fractured.

Wentworth thought it was not. God knows he had felt often enough the prodding fury of violent lead to be able to calculate shock. If the bone had been hit by .38 calibre lead, his legs probably would have been hammered straight out from under him. *Not* broken then… He lay motionless and heard the triumphant shouting of the police, heard the rapid beat of feet toward him. If they came close enough….

The footsteps stopped a scant stride away. "Get up from there, you!" a cop's voice panted. "Come on, I just pinked you in the leg. Get up, damn it!"

Wentworth did not stir and another man tromped up beside the first, came to a halt. "Maybe he hit his head when he fell," he muttered. "I'll get the cuffs on him. You hold that gun ready."

Wentworth made his body remain limp. The cobblestones were cool to his friction-burned flesh, soothing to his cheek. His breath came in long, shuddering gasps that swelled his ribs. The cop came cautiously nearer and Wentworth heard the tinkle of the handcuff chain, the burr of the ratchet as they were opened. A hand clamped on his wrist and, with the quickness of a snake, Wentworth's hand snatched up to seize the cop's wrist. He rolled… toward the man! His back struck the man's shin, pinned his feet and drove him violently backward toward the cobbles. There was a muffled shout, the crash of a gun!

Wentworth felt the sear of powder-flame, but no fresh shock… then he was on his feet. A violent leap, a fierce shout from his tightened throat and he had hammered aside the leveling gun. His fist drove into the policeman's jaw, then again. The second man went down, but the first already was struggling to rise, to draw his gun. Wentworth stooped to speed his fist home, and rose with the arching hook of the uppercut. It did the work, and he could race on. His wounded leg gave under him at each stride and the pain was starting like a hot iron running up through his fibers.

Wentworth ground his fist into the wound, raced on. More guns now; more shouting police and the pound of footsteps, but he was within a few yards of his car. There was time now to leap behind the wheel, to jab the key into the ignition lock. He kicked the starter with a bare heel, whipped the car in a tight U-turn and was racing ahead of the foremost cops. They stopped their chase, one of them dropped to his knee with a gun leveled across a forearm for accuracy. Wentworth whipped the wheel over, almost wrecked the car in straightening out again; swerved again and made the corner!

For a half dozen blocks, he raced at top speed, then slammed the car into an alleyway and set about exploring the wound in his thigh. The bullet had drilled straight through, and the hole was small… a cupro-nickel bullet probably. His hand snapped to the kit he always carried in the car and iodine bit into the raw flesh. Wentworth's teeth gritted at the pain; his body sagged back against the cushions and there was a spasm he could not control in the tortured thigh muscles. Presently, he could straighten and start the bandaging. The wound had bled freely, would be clean… if he was lucky.

Fumblingly, Wentworth reached behind the seat and drew out a suit-box. There was no clothing here save the disguise of the Spider, but there were shoes, and a shirt. He forced his swollen feet into the leather, drew on the shirt. It would have to serve.

He delayed a few instants longer to examine the papers he had taken from the body of the priest who had attempted to murder him in the secret room. His eyes blurred as he studied them, and shock ran through him when he realized their contents. There could be no doubt. The man he had knocked out, who had afterward been killed, was the secret agent of a powerful European nation! Good Lord, did that mean that the desolation of the flame was being loosed upon the people as a hostile move against the United States?

No time to think about that now. He sent the coupé backward and his hands felt weak upon the wheel. He checked to take a long pull from a brandy flask, and the pallor of his cheeks diminished a little, his head cleared. His lips set thinly, and he turned the coupé about—and headed back toward the Temple of Vishnu, toward the scores of police who would be questing for him now. Dangerous for the Spider? It was more than that. It was almost certain death, either in the fires of Vishnu or at the points of police guns! Yet Wentworth did not hesitate, for his course and his duty lay plainly before him and from that path, the Spider had never yet turned aside!

COMMISSIONER SANFORD DANE was white-faced with fury. His belligerent underlip was shot forward and the police dropped back from his pounding path through the Temple of Vishnu and dared not volunteer speech. He reached the portals just as Kalki was being thrust into the prison van.

The two policemen whom Wentworth had knocked out were being helped heavily to their feet by companions.

When Dane heard their report, he spoke for the first time. "Suspended, pending investigation!" he bit out. "Turn in your shields and guns at once." He spun on his heel. "My car!"

The sergeant, a few strides behind him, piped on his whistle and the chauffeur shot Dane's powerful limousine up beside the van. Dane leaned in and ripped out the microphone of the two-way radio with which it was equipped, began to hammer out orders. Within two minutes, all available radio cars in the district and all station reserves would be speeding into the district. When he had finished, he stood glowering toward the van. Kalki was still thundering out his condemnations.

"Silence that man," Dane shouted. "Silence him, if you have to bludgeon him!"

Through the doorway, the flicker of a whirled nightstick glinted and there was the dull crack of its contact... and Kalki was silent. The prison van started for headquarters and, before the doors of the temple, Dane stood with his thick legs braced and his close-clipped head pulled forward, glaring.

The van lurched slowly across South Street. As it passed the spot where Wentworth had fallen, wounded, an ominous thing happened. Flame sprang into life on the granite cobbles. It fanned to a high point of yellow and red, remote and thin against the bright light of day and burned steadily through a count of ten, then flickered and went out! If any man on the van saw it, he paid no heed. The police dared not speak to Commissioner Dane and his eyes, reddened with anger, stared out fixedly across the street. Kalki had said, *"The flames shall follow us through the streets and your people shall die!"*

The prison van entered the street where Wentworth's car had been parked. There were no people here. Slowly, the van jolted on… and there were people ahead.

There were the sprawling tenements of the slums, stirred early to life. Laboring men with black pipes between the teeth, lifted their incurious eyes to see the van come toward them, and plodded on with their perpetually weary feet. A girl in a brief skirt, a pert hat on the back of crisply curled hair, flicked down the stone steps of a building and hurried off along the street. A boy darted out of another house to join her, and her hand went through his arm, her mouth was laughing… off to work. So early, there were children in the streets, brawling over a game of "one-old-cat." And the van had almost reached the tenements….

A peddler rolled his pushcart out of a narrow alley, let it thump over the curb and bent his back to the task. He was young and under the pushed-up brim of his old cap, his hair was bright yellow. He puckered his lips and whistled cheerily. When a boy snatched an apple and ran, he bellowed with anger… but only until the boy was out of sight, and then he burst into a happy laugh. Because the peddler was moving toward the river markets, the slow-moving prison van with its cargo of police, with its imprisoned prophet of Vishnu, reached him first.

Laughter and whistle faded from his lips at sight of the big black truck with its solid sides and narrow barred windows. For his kind, the van could mean only trouble and he scowled, and clicked his thumbnail on his teeth toward the police car. *Zut* to the police! They'd grabbed up some poor devil. Rich guys didn't ride in the Black Maria, even when they were arrested. The cop behind the wheel scowled back at him, and the prison van rolled past with a faint mutter of its exhaust—and for a few moments, nothing happened.

Nothing that is except, as the peddler turned to glare after the truck, he felt his eyes water and dashed a hand angrily across them. He bent once more to the task of pushing his cart, but curiously, his eyes still hurt. He ground a knuckle into them and swore in bewilderment. The curse rose thinly in his throat, broke—and it was just afterward that he screamed for the first time.

He tore at his eyes and from behind his blunt, calloused fists, little darts of red thrust out. They wrapped in between his fingers, pushing out strongly, lapping eagerly at the fuel of his eyes!

THE CHILDREN weren't frightened, not yet. They saw the peddler rub his eyes; they even saw the first of the flames lick out between his hardy fingers, and they thought it was some trick he was doing to amuse them. Antonio was full of tricks like that, a nice guy. He didn't even get sore when you swiped his fruit, if you didn't take too much. There was a sort of understanding between them about that.

The children ran toward him, calling to each other in excitement, laughing already in anticipation of Antonio's trick. This was a good one, all right; those flames licking out like that. But Antonio was a fool to cover up his eyes. Those big ripe bananas, those luscious red apples were swell grub and their stomachs were never too well filled.

They flocked around Antonio, laughing at him, kidding him along. Those screams sounded just like the real thing. They sort of made a cold chill run up your back....

"Look, Antonio's dancing!"

"Funny kind of dance. What's he bending over like that for?"

"Antonio's got a pain in his belly!"

"Hey, Antonio!"

Antonio was flat on his stomach on the pavement. He drummed his feet like a child in a tantrum, and the screams were muffled. His tearing nails left streaks of red on his cheeks; streaks of blood, and the flames—the jubilant little flames— trickled along. They sprang out of the creases of his neck, tiny flickering points of red and gold and where they touched the flesh crinkled and turned brown, turned black.

"Hey! Hey, *Antonio!*"

"Say! That ain't no trick. That ain't..."

The flames grew bolder. They swept across Antonio's bright yellow hair and left his head black and smoking, and still the man writhed, still he screamed—and death, blessed death, would not come....

It was because of Antonio's trick that the children did not notice the smarting in their own eyes. It was just when they finally realized the horror on the concrete pavement at their feet, when they turned to flee, that the first boy let out a suffering shriek.

A shriek answered the cry of the boy and a woman began to

wail. She jumped back from the window and, instants later, her feet hammered heavily on the rickety steps. Too late, minutes too late… Giorgio was writhing on the pavement and the flames—those happy, crackling little flames—did their dance of fury, of torture over his prostrate form. The children were scattering everywhere; running in desperation, but they carried their death with them, in their stinging eyes, in the dry mouths.

And the prison van rolled on….

It was passing the transfixed girl in her pert hat and her swinging brief skirts; passing the boy to whose arm she clung while they stared at the horror they could not understand.

But they did not stare long. The flames took care of that. The boy tried to smother the fire with his arms, with his tortured chest. There was a little red tongue that ran straight up the middle of his back. It started from nowhere, a little hesitant point of fire, but presently it swelled furiously. It enveloped them both, where they lay; it roared straight up into the air, for there was fuel in plenty in those young, quivering bodies. There was a… *smell*, and the sound of *frying*….

THE POLICE on the van stared and did not understand. It was the first time they had seen the fires of hell, but they remembered the threats that this queer big man with the fiery red hair had uttered. They stared toward him, and toward the street along which the red death spread swiftly, and their faces went pale, went ashy gray. One man crossed himself and another bent over and began to slap the face of Kalki, the avatar of Vishnu.

He was white-faced.

"Hey!" he yelled, his voice thin. "Hey, wake up! You've got to stop this stuff. You're killing people! Hey...."

The driver of the van twisted around to stare back through the narrow latticed port behind him. "Hey what's the matter? Hey..." He saw the flames and his voice died. "Golly! Oh, Golly..." He jammed his foot down on the accelerator and the engine began to roar; the truck hammered through the streets and, as it fled, the flames popped up....

Two blocks ahead, a battered coupé was speeding along the street and, at the siren's yelp, a strained, sharp-lined face turned to peer back. The man's lips drew thin together and a curse beat against them. God, he had thought to race ahead of that prison van. He had hoped the criminals would be ahead, spreading their flaming death, and he had erred. He had erred terribly!

The coupé whipped aside and Wentworth's hand flicked to the automatic tucked into his waistband. It seemed madness, but he could not doubt the evidence of his eyes. By the heavens, the flames were following the prison van, even as Kalki had threatened! In God's name, what was this horror that the mere passage of the van that carried Kalki could spread to torment and slay the people?

Wentworth could not guess at the answer, but one thing he knew. This prison van must be stopped, before it spread the horror over half the city. The van careened past, lunging over the hum-mocked pavement and Wentworth swerved into its wake. The automatic was easy in his hand and, very deliberately, he lifted it. He saw the frantic men in the back of the van. There was one blue-coated policeman on his knees, with his hands clasped before him, and even as Wentworth spotted him, he heard a woman on the pavement scream, saw her begin the torture dance of the flames; the torment that could end only in death.

Wentworth emptied the automatic in a swift drumroll. He could afford to take no chances on a miss. He saw the right rear wheel, at which he had aimed, leap to the explosion of the tire, and then settle; saw the truck swerve wildly as it felt the jar of the blow-out. The police were staring toward him, and their bewildered daze left them swiftly. Here was something they could understand, something they could combat... a man with a gun. They got in each other's way in their eagerness to wrench out their own weapons and open fire.

That instant's delay was Wentworth's salvation. His car was already rolling at high speed. Without waiting to see the ultimate result of his shot, he stepped hard on the accelerator and sent the coupé surging toward the truck. He swerved wide around its left side and the guns bellowed an instant too late. He whipped past the truck, saw the driver fighting the wheel; saw it lunge over the curb and swerve to as it sideswiped the wall to grind to a halt against the stone steps of a tenement.

The driver was bent hard forward over the wheel, but as Wentworth peered into his rear-vision mirror, he saw the man lift himself stiffly. Wentworth sucked in a breath of relief. The man was not injured seriously.

Wentworth whipped his coupé around the corner and, on the opposite side of the block, swerved to the curb. He was out instantly and ducking into a tenement house. As he raced through the corridor, he was reloading his automatic. He bounded across the rear court, then slowed, moving quietly toward the street where the wrecked van had pulled to a halt. There was a knife frown between his eyes and he blinked experimentally, waiting for the smarting that might herald his own death.

He knew now that the pain came first to the eyes. He had seen too many die under the flames of Vishnu not to know that. But there was no pain. It was a thing he could not understand. The death followed the prison van, and yet the men on it were not affected; Kalki was not harmed—and he himself, who had sprinted directly in its wake, felt no warning pain. There must be some explanation for that. Kalki, of course, would have been rendered immune. That was essential, but the others, himself....

He checked his thought, peering out into the street. The police stood around the wrecked truck and Kalki was dizzily on his feet, hands manacled before him, four police close about him with their drawn guns. Wentworth's gun-hand twitched. But, damn it, the man had been unconscious throughout the trip! The sergeant was plodding purposefully toward a small delivery truck, parked at the curb. The driver popped out of a store, started toward it... and stopped at the sergeant's call.

"I'm commandeering that truck," the sergeant snapped. "You will drive."

His gesture brought the men with Kalki quickly to the rear of the truck and they boosted the massive body inside. Wentworth hesitated. Somewhere about the prison van must be the secret of the flame death. Should he stay to overcome the police and learn that secret—or should he trail Kalki to headquarters.

Surely, Kalki could spread no death from a commandeered truck. Something must have been done to the van. It had to be that. No man—not even an avatar of Vishnu—Wentworth's lips twisted in mockery at the memory of that golden shrine—could call death out of the thin air. It wasn't possible, damn it!

WENTWORTH REMAINED quietly in the shadows of the doorway, his eyes shifting from the grocery truck to the prison van… and suddenly an oath leaped from his lips! There in the shadow of the prison van's driving cab, there was a small sparkle of flame! Even as Wentworth stared, the fire brightened, ran in a quick, bright circle around the rim of the steering wheel. Wentworth leaped from the door with some mad idea of extinguishing the fire before the secret of those flames could be obliterated—but in the same moment, it was too late. The cushions were blazing. There was a muffled blast, and the entire van was a roiling mass of flames!

Through a long minute, Wentworth stood staring at the doomed truck, then he turned and went heavily back into the doorway of the tenement. The police were shouting about the blaze. One of them ran toward the store, but no fire equipment could save it now. Damn it, the fiends were too clever. The last trace of their activities would be blotted out. No choice for Wentworth save to trail Kalki to headquarters, to hope—no, to dread—that the flames of Vishnu would follow him, to hunt down the men who spread it so terribly.

Wentworth was limping heavily as he moved back toward his coupé. Under the heat of the battle, he had driven his muscles to fierce effort, and he was paying the penalty. The pain of the wound ate upward feverishly. He had to rest it, or he would be out of the battle for days—days when the flames of Vishnu could ravish the city unchecked.

There was a weariness upon Wentworth as he climbed back into his coupé and tucked the automatic into his waistband, but his senses remained alert. He spotted the sleek limousine of Sanford Dane as it turned the corner and whispered toward him, took his eyes quickly away, and bent toward the ignition switch. Probably, Dane would not even glance toward the coupé. Yet there was a chance he would—that he would identify the man who had stood before him imprinting the Spider's seal. Wentworth thought grimly that there was much more than a chance. Dane was not the kind of man to forget an indignity like Wentworth's escape.

Out of his eye-corners he watched Dane whom he could see vaguely through the closed windows of the limousine, could make out the glowering, harsh lines of his belligerent face. And he saw Dane suddenly jerk erect—saw his hand reach out to rap the glass behind his chauffeur. Before the man could more than turn his head to get the meaning of Dane's call, Wentworth kicked the starter and wrenched the coupé violently from the curb.

The limousine veered toward him. He saw the driver's set, determined face, caught the glint of a drawn gun flashing into Dane's hand. Wentworth hurled his coupé straight at the limousine, his eyes battling with those of the police chauffeur. He saw the man's hands twitch hesitantly at the steering wheel and, at the last possible moment, Wentworth threw his coupé in the opposite direction, ripped by with his powerful engine roaring in second gear.

Wentworth had thought to gain at least two blocks while the police limousine maneuvered into a turn, but the chauffeur was quick. He threw the front wheels up on the sidewalk, whipped about and made the turn in a swift whirl that scraped fenders on building walls on opposite sides of the street… but lost not so much as two seconds in the chase.

Wentworth's gray-blue eyes tightened in sudden realization that he was in for a hard chase. He flicked on his radio and, instantly, caught the hammer of Dane's deep voice, snapping out orders over the two-way radio system. And there were a multitude of extra cars wedged into the district by his previous instructions. This time, Dane would do a thorough job of it. There was personal animosity as well as his duty to drive him on! THE QUICK brain of the Spider recognized at once that his only hope of eluding the multiple pursuit that was getting underway would be to get out of the district immediately. Manhattan had suddenly become a place of narrow runways, from which there was no escape. Dane was already closing the bridges and the tunnels, was throwing a web of intercepting cars up before and behind him, to north and to south.

Wentworth was not troubled by the danger of the limousine overtaking him. His own engine, masked under that decrepit paint job, was a hundred and seventy-five horsepower. Also, he could make sharper turns than Dane's car, but against the blocking tactics of the police he was almost helpless. For the Spider did not war on the police!

Wentworth threw the wheel over at the first northward street and ground down on the accelerator. The motor hurled him forward at break-neck speed, and the houses flew past toward the rear. Fortunately, traffic was still light. He hammered through traffic signals with blaring horn, switched on the super-charger. If only he had had time to reload the chemical reservoir under the hood and could spurt out a smoke-screen, there might be more chance of a getaway. There had been no time. There had been only ceaseless battle, pursuit and escape.

Two blocks ahead, he saw a radio car rocket into his path. He stamped on the brake, stood up behind the wheel to sweep into a side street. The tires whined. They shrieked. The coupé was heeled far over and the curb was dangerously close. If his wheels hit that, broadside... He wrenched more power into the engine, and the tires caught, sent him hurtling ahead. The limousine screamed into the curb behind him, and its greater weight glued it to the pavement. Wentworth was aware of open, shrieking faces on the sidewalks, but no sound reached his ears save the thunder of his engine and the hissing hurricane of the wind. He was within fifty feet of the corner, when he saw a radio car whip past. He swore, but there was nothing for it but to grind more speed out of the engine and hope....

He bolted across the street and a truck swerved violently from his path, jolted its front wheels over the curb before it stopped. The radio car, a wild glimpse of the passing street showed Wentworth, already was whirling about, but it was behind. It could be forgotten. It could almost be forgotten. Unless they got a clear space to loose their machine-gun... Wentworth turned northward once more. He was on Madison. Too congested. Couldn't hope to make speed here... Radio cars yelped on his trail; the hammer of Dane's voice, shouting changing orders into the radio, plotting out the course Wentworth must follow, throwing more cars into his course.

"You won't be able to stop him without gunfire," Dane was saying savagely. "Do not hesitate to shoot to kill. It is the Spider!"

The echoing beat of the engine against the houses, broken only by the momentary slackening when streets were passed, seemed to hammer out words, too. Swift, deadly words. "The Spider... Shoot to kill!"

Wentworth was weaving a frantic way through traffic, dodging blundering buses, sending his piercing gaze far ahead to ferret out the blockades of the police. Squarely in his path, and no more than fifty feet ahead, a big bus suddenly swerved across the street and Wentworth glimpsed a policeman standing beside the driver. Wentworth cut the wheel over, held the accelerator down. Nothing else to do. His fender shrilled against the rear of the bus as he cut to its right. The driver tried to cut back, to squeeze him over the curb, but the coupé was past. The flicker of the powder-flame from the cop's revolver was a blinking point of light in Wentworth's rear-vision mirror.

Radio cars ahead again. One volleyed at him from a side street to his right. The limousine was blocked for a moment by the maneuvering bus. Wentworth whipped over toward Fifth Avenue, slammed into a side street and a shout of consternation surged to his lips! This was no part of the police plan, but it was the end. A coal truck was maneuvering backward to the curb, and it completely filled the gap between parked cars. No chance to hit the sidewalk. He was stopped!

Wentworth stood on the brake, jerked on the emergency. The coupé bucked like an untamed horse. It see-sawed as he grimly fought the wheel and, behind, the sirens were triumphant.

Wentworth punched open the door and leaped to the pavement while his coupé slammed on against the truck, hiked up its rear end and dropped it with a double blast of exploded tires. Wentworth's wounded leg gave way and he went down, rolling, was up in a trice and hurling himself at a head-long sprint past the coal truck, on toward Fifth Avenue. A gun banged once behind him, and the truck driver shouted and lunged toward Wentworth. A leap took Wentworth even with the driver and he whipped his left in hard to the belly.

"Sorry," Wentworth muttered… and meant it. It was never his desire to hurt innocent men. The truck driver was on the side of the law.

Desperation drew Wentworth's lips long across his face, and his breath whistled through his distended nostrils. There was a wide staring look in his eyes and his body winced each time his wounded leg hit the ground. He could not run far on that leg; but there was no car in sight which he could commandeer. He would win a short respite because of the blockading coal truck, but it would be a matter of seconds only before the police rounded that truck and their guns began.

Wentworth drove himself mercilessly. Before that time, he must be far enough ahead so that their aim would be unsure. He *must*… His eyes shuttled from side to side of the street, desperately. These shops offered no protection. Few of them had rear exits and he could not be sure, if he made a choice, that he would be lucky. His luck had been slim this day. God, this could not be the end. He was needed too badly. The flames of Vishnu....

It was despair that brought the oath to his lips, an oath that was half prayer. Into the opposite end of the street, dead ahead, a police car whirled. His escape was cut off! Behind him... behind him, there was a shout, and the first police gun crashed!

Was this the end?

CHAPTER 6
DEATH TO THE SPIDER!

TO AVOID those first wild bullets, Wentworth flung himself sideways, close against the line of parked cars which had helped to trap him. They offered him now at least a partial protection from the guns of his pursuers. It could not last. Soon the police would leap to the sidewalk, and after that he must take to the street. And there would be men there, too. There were those two in the radio car ahead. As the thought crossed his brain, the two radio cops sprang to the street and went into action. One of them darted toward the pavement to head Wentworth off, and the other took his stand in the street, long-barreled revolver lifted and ready in his fist!

Surrender was unthinkable. While guns and voices of anger hounded him, Wentworth sprang between two of the parked cars, whipped out his gun and fired three shots high over the heads, of the police. That would slow them up. They would think he was making a stand here between the cars. Every second gained helped him toward escape. He thrust the gun away, flung himself prone upon the pavement... and crawled under the machine ahead! There was only room to worm along on his belly.

Ragged bolt ends and pins snagged at his shoulders, twice scraped his scalp. He dragged his wounded leg, squirmed along on his side with the help of his right foot, his hands. His old army training stood him in good stead and he covered ground at amazing speed.

He emerged, hidden, from the front of the car, darted under the next, did that three times while the police moved forward cautiously. They shouted orders to surrender. A bullet quested toward the spot from which he had fired. Wentworth plunged under the fourth car, and it was a high-riding old-fashioned machine. The broad black shoes, the stealthy, slow lifting of blue-trousered legs which he could see from his lair, came closer. He heard the two radio police, who were ahead of him, call in hoarse whisper to each other.

"Look under the cars!" one said. "Wait, we better start about two cars back. He couldn't get any farther than that!"

Wentworth nodded, his face grim. Yes, they were the pick of the force, these men who rode the radio cars. They used their heads. But Wentworth had counted on this, and it was for that reason he had paused under the old-fashioned car. He hooked his bad leg, cautiously, over the brake rods, the rear axle, followed it by the right; then set his hands upon a cross-member of the frame and lifted his body, pressed hard against the flooring of the car.

If the police lay prone upon the sidewalk, they could see him… but not otherwise. He could not see them now, could only strain his ears and listen to the slow, furtive rasping of their shoes as they advanced. The heel of one cop's shoe squeaked regularly and Wentworth heard his whispered oath. If they spotted him now….

A gun thudded to the soft asphalt just beside him, and he saw the cop's hands, one gripping the revolver, braced against the pavement. He was going to give the underside of the car a thorough inspection! Wentworth clutched his own revolver. He would not fire, but if the man spotted him, he might reach out and knock him out before he could give the alarm. He held his breath, waiting.

The cop's breath came out noisily as he lowered himself to the pavement. There was a pause, then a grunt that might mean anything at all. Wentworth clutched the automatic, his forearm ached with tension. He dared not look down under the side of the car. Another grunt, and the feet once more made their slow rasping. Wentworth gasped with relief. In an instant, he was free of his hiding place and inching forward, ducked under the next car; the next. The police were well past him. The radio car was not twenty feet ahead… Wentworth grinned, wryly. If he could make that….

TWO MORE cars and he was just beside the parked radio car. He peered cautiously about. The police were searching the last car in the line, the one from behind which he had fired. A moment and they would suspect trickery, renew their search.

Wentworth slid out from behind the parked cars, darted in behind the radio machine. If he could run for it now....

He took a short stride, and a siren whined ahead of him. More radio cars coming! Then, running was useless. He whipped about—and climbed into the radio car! Soft laughter pushed at his lips. There was a pair of handcuffs lying behind the seat. As quick as thought, he snatched them up and laid them over his right wrist, but so loosely that he could slip it off over his hand. He snapped the other end tightly about the doorpost and sat there, his head pulled forward sullenly, a scowl on his face!

The radio car he had heard swept into the street, raced forward until blocked by the car in which Wentworth sat. The cops jumped out, ranged forward. One of them whipped his head toward the car where Wentworth sat, jerked to a halt. Wentworth sat unmoving, staring sullenly back at him, and rattled the handcuffs slightly.

"Well, what you looking at?" he grumbled. "Think this is a zoo?"

"You said it, monkey-face!" the cop grinned. "Don't run off with those handcuffs!" He loped on, and the other cop ran beside him toward the spot where other police were searching beneath the cars.

Wentworth sucked in a slow, relieved breath. As he had dared to hope, the police had mistaken him for a prisoner already captured and handcuffed to the car to await the pleasure of the radio cops, while they searched for someone else. He was safe in this spot as long as the actual operators of the car did not come... or until one of the new arrivals mentioned seeing him. Meantime, the sun glare on the windshield would hide him from the searchers a half-block away.

Wentworth twisted cautiously to peer behind him. There was the usual crowd of citizens at the end of the block, staring toward the police, but the occasional crash of guns had held them back so far. No cops there that Wentworth could see. He freed his hand of the cuff and slipped once more behind the radio car toward the second parked machine. Its motor was purring softly. If he could reach that, perhaps....

He was just beside it when he heard a shout from the police and a gun crashed again. Frenziedly, he flung himself behind the wheel, wrenched the car into reverse and shot it backward up the street. He made the corner and the crowd split to let him through. A quick maneuver and he was racing up Fifth Avenue. His siren sent traffic scuttling to the curb. But it could not last. His radio brought the sharp voice of Sanford Dane, telling the police what had happened, spreading the net.

"Stop him at any price. Ram the car!" Dane was snarling.

As if in echo of that voice, a radio car plunged like a projectile from the side street just ahead. It wavered for a moment, then the wheels straightened... and it headed straight for Went-

NITA VAN SLOAN —

worth's car! He could glimpse the driver's face, set and white; see the tension of his hands upon the wheel. No question but that he meant to obey the commissioner literally.

Wentworth whipped his eyes over the street and a gasp of thankfulness surged to his throat. He was only a half block from the twin apartment buildings where Nita van Sloan had apartments. She had a suite in each structure and even the management did not know that both were hers... or of the secret door and dressing-room which Nita, with the help of Wentworth's

87

servitors and comrades-at-arms, had constructed. If he could just reach it... The key was always in the leather girdle he wore.

The radio car was less than fifty feet away, and headed unswervingly toward him. Wentworth jammed the accelerator to the floor and headed for a narrow break between two parked cars. The radio machine would not quite squeeze through, he knew, but it was better than a head-on collision. That fool driver... The radio car leaped under the spur of Wentworth's foot. There was a tearing clash of ripping fenders and the car wedged itself into the opening.

In an instant, Wentworth had hurled himself head-first through the open right window, away from the charging radio car. He slid across the hood of the parked limousine, got his hands on the pavement and dragged his legs afterward. He bit down a cry of pain as his wounded leg struck the sidewalk, then he was up and running, bent double behind the cars.

THE CRASH of guns beat time for his feet, but he knew his goal and did not swerve from it. He lunged through the pretentious doors of the apartment house, latticed in ornate bronze work, and the glass crashed to the stab of a bullet. An attendant stared with open mouth, and Wentworth leaped past him to the elevator. It was an automatic and the door slid laboriously shut just as the attendant recovered and leaped to stop him. But the cage was crawling upward.

Wentworth shifted his feet restlessly. His whole body was thrust forward, tensely, waiting for the stop. With his wound, there was no time to go to the wrong floor and attempt to confuse the police. He would have to risk that. His hand rested flatly against the wound on his thigh and he stared down at a scattering of dark red drops upon the floor! Lord, he had to stop that!

Swiftly, he tore off his shirt and tied it, trailing, about his ankle to catch the seepage of blood. He tore off his shoe and stood ready when the elevator's slow mechanical door began to slide open. He punched the button for the top floor, squeezed through, shouldered open the outer door and limped along the hall. He peered anxiously behind him. He had left no trace, thanks to his precautions. The light was burning beneath the outer control button of the elevator, but whether it was going up or down, he could not tell now.

He fumbled out the key, lunged into the apartment, along a neat hall to a bedroom; then into the bath. He stepped into the shower and whipped the curtain closed, then he turned toward a design worked into the tile sidewall. He put his thumb on the sail of a blue-tile ship, and his middle finger upon a leaping dolphin. He put the heel of his left hand upon an unmarked white tile which he located by a swift count, then he pressed upon the three points in rotation, twice. A door swung open in the tile....

Wentworth staggered through the opening, whipped the shower curtain aside and leaned his shoulder against the door to close it. He... Why, good lord, he was on his hands and knees on the floor! So tired. He slipped down, cushioned his cheek on the soft rug and... darkness.

The mutter of voices stirred him back to full consciousness and he made out the hoarsely angry tones in which Commissioner Dane seemed always to speak. Swiftly, Wentworth pushed his weary body to his feet. His wounded leg had stiffened and he barely bit down a groan as he crossed to a listening device and threw a tumbler which brought him clearly the words of the men in the other room.

"Damn it, man," Dane's voice came shortly. "The fingerprint powder shows he ran with one shoe off straight to this room. There's a print in the bottom of the tub, and you tell me you can find nothing. I tell you there's a secret room hidden here somewhere and it's up to you to find it!"

Wentworth swore in amazement. Dane was proving cleverer than he had thought! Lucky that he always coated his fingers with collodion these days, lest an accidental print betray him. They would find no trace of his touching the tiles. Even if they did, it would not avail them unless they pressed them in the right rotation, and with the curtain drawn shut.

"Dust that tile," Dane said shortly. "If he touched that…."

Wentworth thrust himself away from the listening device, let the tumbler snap back into place. That would show them nothing, but if Dane's mind worked that way, he would quickly hit on the possibility of a connection with the next building. And Nita's suite was just beyond the wall! Or he might try the more direct means of using axes and sledgehammers on the wall!

Wentworth let his hand rest briefly against the sheet steel that walled the room. It would take an acetylene torch to drive a way through that, but it could be done. Afterward, they would find the door that led through into Nita's apartment, and she would be linked irrevocably to the Spider! Wentworth flung himself at the dressing-table across the room, dropped into the seat. It would take a considerable time to achieve the fracture of that steel wall, but meantime he must contrive a way to spare Nita. God, he had been mad to take refuge here. Mad!

SWIFT APPLICATION of a fluid Wentworth himself had prepared swiftly removed the makeup from his face and brought out the lean, aristocratic line of his own features. He wrenched off the long wig, the false eyebrows and nothing was left of the street musician at all.

For a long moment, Wentworth stared blankly at his own face in the mirror. The gray-blue eyes were narrow in thought, and the line of the mouth was uncompromising. Abruptly, he laughed, and the mocking line of his brows accentuated, the lines of his face filled. It was once more the countenance of Richard Wentworth, dilettante of the arts and amateur dabbler in criminology, and it was the humor of Wentworth that smiled out of the fine eyes.

"I am very forgetful," he murmured, "This is Jenkyns' day off!"

He set swiftly to work upon his face, applying a coloring liquid that turned it ruddy, and then another that puckered the flesh like the withering hand of age. A skillful shadow pencil subtly accentuated the wrinkles and then he turned his attention to his hands. He did not dare trust to wearing gloves; not with Dane's newly discovered keenness over details opposed to him. He heightened the blueness of the veins. By clenching his fists hard, he could make them swell a little as with age, and the same fluid that had wrinkled his face would age his hands.

Skillfully, he applied white, heavy brows over his own, drew on a wig of crisp, curly silver hair and secured it with spirit gum. He was nearly ready. He stripped the clothing from his hard, lean body, bent anxiously to examine the wound in his thigh. It was red, inflamed. He had to rest it, or there might be trouble.

The sudden thudding jar of axes on the wall jerked him erect. No time even to think about that now. He put on a new bandage and rapidly dressed. Ten minutes after he had thrown himself at the dressing-table, he stood, fully clothed in the formal morning garb of a butler... Hard to realize that it was still only morning! The stiff formality of a butler's bearing would help him to conceal the injury to his leg. But if Dane once suspected him....

Wentworth shook the thought from his brain. He must make sure that there was no suspicion aroused! He made a rapid pile of the clothing he had discarded, spread inflammable liquid over it. Then he crossed to a closet equipped with drawers and a neat laboratory bench and his fingers moved with deft speed among the bottles.

In five minutes, he had contrived to fill eight small metal containers with fluid. He placed them carefully about the secret room, in the wardrobe, in the laboratory. He put three about the secret door into Nita's apartment. That must be obliterated so that there was nothing left to prove that there had been a door. He peered through into the music room, where the secret door opened, and it was empty. Now everything was prepared.

With a swift, final look at himself in the mirrors, Wentworth tossed a handful of bullets upon the heaped up, fuel-soaked clothing, struck a match to the pile... and opened the secret door into Nita's apartment. As he swiftly closed the door behind him, hermetically sealing off the secret room, he heard the faint, distant whirr of the doorbell.

Wentworth settled his clothing and drew himself up stiffly. The humor went from his face and it was the blank countenance of a butler. It was more than that. The entire secret of Wentworth's expert capacity for disguise lay in the mind of the man. When he put on a disguise, he ceased to be Richard Wentworth and became, literally, in thought as well as in appearance, the man he was simulating. Now he was a butler. The door bell was whirring again, and being an aged butler, he was angry at the presumptuousness of a person who would ring twice on such short notice. He put on hauteur like a glove and stalked toward the main door of the apartment.

IN THE drawing room, a tall, turbaned Sikh was taking long, barefoot strides toward the entrance hallway. He turned his full-bearded, dark face at the sound of Wentworth's step and now his eyes widened.

"*Wah*, Jenkyns," he said, "I thought you had gone."

Wentworth said, with Jenkyns' dignity, and in his old deep, worried voice. "I did not feel so well, Ram Singh. And you are careless in attending to Miss Nita's wants. The master would want me to watch over her."

Ram Singh's white teeth flashed behind his beard and Wentworth passed him toward the door. Relief flooded through him. If he could thus easily fool Ram Singh, who knew him so well… The doorbell whirred again. Wentworth opened it, and his face was stiff with Jenkyns' disapproval. There was a uniformed policeman.

"Really, my dear man," Wentworth said haughtily. "There is no need to keep ringing so violently. You disturb people."

The cop was daunted; it made his cheeks flush angrily. "Sure, the law can wait," he rumbled. "Listen, I'm searching the place."

"Of course you have a warrant?" Wentworth said haughtily. "In the absence of my mistress, I cannot permit...."

The cop shouldered his way in. "Listen, there ain't no question of a warrant. We chased a crook into this place and we're coming after him. Maybe you never heard of the Spider?"

"Ram Singh!" Wentworth lifted his voice, making it shake with indignation.

The tall Sikh stepped quietly into the hallway behind Wentworth, his powerful arms folded across his chest. His eyes rested hostilely upon the policeman.

"I am here, Jenkyns," he said softly.

"This officer demands the right to search without a warrant," Wentworth said testily. "Under the circumstances, he has no more right here than any other trespasser. You would be entirely justified...."

"Hey, wait!" the cop backed up. "Hey, wait, there ain't going to be no rough stuff now. I just asked peaceable...."

"You asked nothing, my man," Wentworth said coldly. "You asserted your right. Now, if the mistress permits...."

"Sure, sure," the cop said hurriedly. "Just ask her, that's all."

Wentworth hesitated. Surely, Nita was not here or the sounds of disturbance would have brought her to see the trouble. She had lived too much in the presence of danger to ignore any unusual thing. He opened his lips... and saw Commissioner

Dane step around a corner of the hall where, plainly, he had been listening.

If Commissioner Dane insisted, Wentworth knew that he could not much longer resist without attracting suspicion to himself, yet he dared not let them in. Undoubtedly, they would go directly to the spot behind which they knew the secret room was situated. And it was almost time for the explosion. At any moment, one of those bullets would discharge from the heat and when they did, the eight bombs he had placed about the room would discharge simultaneously. They were filled with the powerful explosive which was Wentworth's secret—the Spider's secret—and there were three of them just beyond the wall where the men would be standing!

If the Spider had been the merciless killer the police seemed to think him, that would not have mattered, but he never took innocent lives—and as surely as Dane went to that spot, so surely would he be killed by the discharge of that awful blast!

Dane confronted him, lower lip thrust out, close-clipped head pulled down belligerently. "One side, man," he said sharply. "I am Commissioner Dane and I assume full responsibility."

"I will take your message to my mistress," Wentworth told him gravely, "but I cannot...."

The words died on his lips. Tinkling through the apartment came the slow silvery notes of the piano... and the instrument was less than ten feet from the wall where those incredibly powerful bombs awaited the moment of discharge. The piano... and it was Nita's lovely, delicate hands that were tripping over the keys. It could be no one else!

"I will hurry," Wentworth said, with difficulty.

He turned away from the door and took deliberate steps toward the portieres that draped the entrance to the drawing-room, beyond which was the arch of the music chamber. Once out of Dane's sight, he could run, could snatch Nita from the path of peril. Dane could be taken care of afterward, and....

"I will accompany you," Dane said shortly, and his feet beat their heavy, deliberate way in Wentworth's wake!

WENTWORTH PINCHED back an oath. He could not run now, without betraying himself. If he did not, Nita—sweet, brave Nita—would die! Perhaps there was another way. There had to be. Wentworth whirled to confront Commissioner Dane.

"I cannot permit this!" he said, and made his voice quaver high with indignation. "I am not at all sure that Miss Nita can receive you and your ruffian police! I do not care if you are the Commissioner of Police. You are a mannerless ruffian!"

"Giving warning, eh?" Dane snapped.

His thrust against Wentworth's chest sent him staggering backward. He let out a thin, quavering cry as a final warning to Nita, then his wounded leg gave way and he fell heavily to the floor. He heard Nita's quiet voice, saw that she had come to the doorway of the music room and relief loosened all his muscles. She would be safe in here.

Dane was striding toward her, and Wentworth scrambled to his feet. There were four of the uniformed police in the room now—two plainclothesmen. But Wentworth's eyes went hauntingly to Nita. She wore a morning gown of soft blue and the crisp ringlets of her chestnut hair curled about her shapely head. The line of her chin was haughty and indignant.

"Really, Mr. Dane," she said quietly. "I think I must echo Jenkyns' sentiments. You are a mannerless ruffian."

Dane took his straddle-legged stand before her and his words pelted out with the force of bullets.

"You have been suspect before this, Miss van Sloan," he said violently. "Now we find a secret room beyond the walls of your apartment, a room into which we know the Spider went. And your cheeky fool of a butler tried to bar my entrance."

Nita's smile was disdainful as Wentworth moved toward her, making his hands tremble, wavering in his stride as befitted an elderly man so roughly used. "Really, Mr. Dane?" she asked. "A secret room? I'm afraid you've been attending too many motion pictures lately. Or have you been reading detective stories?"

Wentworth was almost beside Nita and he saw the solid, flat lips of Sanford Dane draw downward in a sneer. "Will you stand aside, or shall I put you aside?" he demanded, harshly.

Nita's face paled. There was a disturbance at the door, and the uniformed policeman was hurled to the floor. Through the entrance of the drawing-room, Ram Singh strode, his black beard bristling, his dark eyes hot with anger, just behind him came the broad-shouldered Jackson, who had served Wentworth as chauffeur. Both had automatics in their fists.

"Is it your wish, Miss Nita," Jackson asked quietly, "that we should expel these trespassers?"

Wentworth could scarcely keep himself from throwing an anxious glance toward the music room. He did not want his men to enter into a pitched battle with the police—but for a few minutes longer, Dane must be kept out of the music room. He must!

Nita said, coolly, "It will not be necessary, Jackson. We have nothing to conceal. If Mr. Dane had been able to behave in a gentlemanly manner, there would have been no obstacle at all."

She stepped leisurely aside from the music-room arch. "You will be held accountable for all damages, Mr. Dane. I think the courts will find you a little ridiculous, searching for secret rooms in an apartment house."

Wentworth started toward her, his hand half-reached to catch Dane by the shoulder… and it was too late. Dane stepped across the sill and, in the same instant, Wentworth felt himself caught up by a fierce hot gust of wind and hurled backward. His head seemed to swell to bursting, and all his body achieved a curious light numbness. He had felt concussion before. He knew, even before the tremendous thunder of the explosion hit him, that the bombs had let go!

CHAPTER 7
VISHNU'S ULTIMATUM

I T WAS night before the police finished in the apartment of Nita van Sloan. Commissioner Dane stamped out angrily long before. He had been hurled backward by the blast and, though shaken and furious, had not been hurt. And Wentworth's bombs did their work well. There was nothing at all about the hole torn through the wall of the secret room to show there had been a door there. Flames swept the chamber and left only a shambles for the police to investigate.

Within a half hour after the police had left, Wentworth presented himself to Nita, still in the guise of Jenkyns.

"If you please, Miss Nita," he said gently, imitating the aged butler's voice, "I shall be going out now. Perhaps if I had gone earlier, so much trouble might not have occurred."

Nita smiled up at him from the window seat in the drawing-room. "Nonsense, Jenkyns," she said softly. "You did precisely right…" Her violet eyes wandered off toward the dark of the night toward the city lights beyond, and Wentworth shut his lips grimly against the pull of his heart. "I wonder," she said softly, "where Master Richie disappeared. The police traced him to that room. He couldn't have come through here… Or could he, Jenkyns?"

Wentworth shook his head, "I don't know, Miss Nita. He could have, I suppose."

Nita sighed, "Oh, Jenkyns… He's out there somewhere, hunted by the police. Hiding. It doesn't seem right that we…."

Wentworth's arms ached to hold her, to comfort her. God, it was cruel to have to go through life like this… but it was better so. Safer for Nita. Too many times, she had shared the cruelty of his own fugitive life; had been hurt, even tortured at the hands of criminals who sought to strike him through her. And he could not reveal himself now, lest she be drawn once more into the tangled skeins of crime and vengeance, into the battle against Kalki.

He said, softly, "It is how Master Richie would want it, Miss Nita. I'll be going now."

Nita's eyes were blurred with tears when she turned them toward him again. "Be careful, Jenkyns," she said. "And if you should, by any chance of fate, see him…."

Her voice faded, and Wentworth said, "Yes, miss?"

"Why, tell him that everything goes well. Tell him that if only he would let me help, let me share…" Nita turned away again.

Wentworth's hand reached out and his fingers just touched, lovingly, the little curl that nestled against the curve of her neck. "I'm sure that he knows already, Miss Nita," he said, and turned away sharply lest the temptation be too strong for him.

It was for her own sake, for Nita's sake, he kept telling himself harshly. He almost ran from the room; heard Nita's voice call after him with a sharply rising question in her tones, and hurried on. She would know the truth of his imposture when Jenkyns himself returned, and she would know the reason. He shut the door softly, and went with the feeble pace of an old man downward in the elevator, feeling the throbbing pain of his leg, but aware of a sharper ache in his heart.

Out into the night, where he had no rest and no shelter. The street musician would be suspect now of Kalki's men. Even his coupé was gone, and it would take time to replace it, time and more funds than he could readily put his hand to at this time. And he must rest. A hotel would provide shelter if he maintained his disguise….

He limped heavily along the street toward Sixth Avenue, where he could get luggage and clothing. The sight of a restaurant reminded him that he had not eaten in long hours, and he turned into it, ordered a hurried meal....

RESOLUTELY, HE forced down his heartache for Nita, drove his mind to the problem of ferreting out the secret of the flame of Vishnu; of smashing the criminals who had loosed this plague of horror. He leaned back, half closed his eyes and, with absolute concentration, combed over the events and discoveries of the day.

He had transferred to this clothing the papers taken from the body of the priest in the temple, which had revealed him as the agent of a European power. He had been sure, at first, that this discovery meant that the whole plot of the flames was a hostile action against the United States. Now, it was becoming plain that, equally, the priest could have been a spy against the criminals, intent on obtaining the secret of the flames for use as a weapon of war.

The man's silent secrecy in attacking him, the fact that afterward he had been murdered, obviously by a priest, would support the latter view. Moreover, it was hard to couple the sincerity of Kalki with a mere governmental attack. No, the secret was deeper than that... deeper, and more ominous!

His mind worried once more over the immunity to the flames which apparently he and the police who had entered the temple shared with Kalki... *who had entered the temple!* Wentworth sat erect with the sudden force of that phrase. Why, of course, that explained it! He remembered that the temple was air-conditioned. Obviously, there had been some substance in circulation in the temple, which rendered all who entered it impervious to the flames!

Wentworth had not been conscious of the radio music, vibrating through the restaurant, until suddenly it was cut off and, in its place, there sounded the deep, sonorous voice of Kalki, the avatar of Vishnu!

All the horror beneath the earth
was lit by lurid flame!

"Unbelievers, beware!" Kalki cried, and the radio quivered and blasted under the assault of his powerful voice.

Wentworth whipped about in his chair, for the moment almost convinced that Kalki himself was present in the room. Speech had stopped throughout the restaurant and people twisted also, to stare toward the radio. Kalki paused briefly after those first words, as if he knew the sensation they created, as if he waited to draw the full attention of his audience. Wentworth had time to wonder how the man could have escaped from the police....

"I speak to you, unbelievers," Kalki began again, "with all reasonableness, in utter goodwill. I am Kalki, tenth avatar of Vishnu, who comes to destroy vice and wickedness—and restore the race of mankind to virtue and purity. Today, the vile minions of the temporal authorities tried to seize me. I mean your police. They are dead. Every man of them dead under the scorching lash of the flames of Vishnu! The prison in which they placed me was consumed by the flames! I alone walked out unharmed!"

Wentworth found himself pulled to his feet by the suppressed violence of Kalki's words, by the horror of the picture he conjured up. Flames sweeping through the cell blocks of the prison, destroying men and jail together... and leaving Kalki unharmed! Wentworth forced down an oath of anger, drove himself back into his chair and Kalki's voice pounded on.

"I tell you these things that you may understand, unbelievers, that no power of man can turn me aside from the goal I have fixed! People have died in the streets this day with the flame of Vishnu eating out their eyes, because they will not see the

104

truth; eating out their souls that will not accept the true god! And many more shall die in that same way until all the world worships Vishnu!"

Somewhere in the restaurant a woman screamed. It broke, for the moment, the spell of Kalki's words and people started to their feet, peered about them with suspicious, frightened eyes. Their panic was electric in the air. The spurt of a struck match would have hurled them all, in wild stampede, fighting for escape from the sound of Kalki's voice. It hammered on.

"So, I serve notice upon the people of this city!" Kalki cried. "They shall close all their churches; their profane altars before false gods shall be destroyed! They shall come at the rise of the sun and at the setting of the sun to the temple of Vishnu and worship. If they fail, then the flames of Vishnu shall visit them! This is my ultimatum!

"Because you are blind, I tell you one more thing. Every day that the people shall fail to heed my voice, crying in this darkness of unbelief, I will smite one thousand of the infidels. I shall strike them with the Flames of Vishnu and they shall die, pleading vainly for mercy, writhing under the torment of the scorned god!

"If the blasphemous churches open their doors, they shall be destroyed. Each of your sabbaths, I shall destroy churches, with their entire congregations, until those who survive have seen the light, and the truth."

WENTWORTH WAS on his feet once more, making his way rapidly toward the street. He had no choice now. Kalki, whether he was the leader, or merely the voice of the conspiracy, was proclaiming warfare upon the people. To that there could be only one answer: Kalki must die under the hand of the Spider!

Wentworth cursed himself bitterly that he had failed to slay this monster of the flames when the man was in his power. He must strike the more quickly, the more ruthlessly for that reason! If Kalki only talked long enough, he would reach the broadcast station and then….

Wentworth flung up a hand at a taxi, and tossed the address of the station at the driver while he flicked on the radio to pick up Kalki's boasting words. Kalki must have invaded the station in force, or else… or else the flames had struck before him!

"Think not," Kalki was crying, "that your police or your armies, nor all your miserable hirelings together, can reach me! I have been forced to hide myself from the myrmidons of your faithless gods, but it shall not stop me from dinning the truth in your deaf ears—and it shall not stop the flames of Vishnu!"

Wentworth said, savagely, "Can't you get any more speed out of this wreck?"

The driver said, "I'm hurrying! Geez, that guy must be nuts. But I seen what those flames can do. Might be wise to play along with him, hunh?"

The clangor of fire sirens shrieked through the night, and the thinner wail of police cars. They were speeding in the direction Wentworth had taken. The taxi took the tail of one of the radio cars, and followed it, roaring, through the split traffic. And still Kalki's voice pounded on.

"Hunt me, you who dare!" Kalki flung out his challenge. "And the flames of Vishnu shall receive you. The true god will protect me! And his fires shall consume any who come seeking with evil in their hearts, with hostile intent toward Kalki, who is Vishnu himself, who is all-powerful and all-conquering!"

Wentworth's eyes were straining ahead and there was a red glow against the night sky that leaped and waned and towered higher; there was rolling black smoke!

"Bow down, fools!" cried Kalki. "Worship while yet there is time. I have been patient, but the time of patience is near an end. Bow down, for the judgment of Vishnu is upon you! Terrible is the wrath of Vishnu!"

The voice died out and afterward there was silence on the air—silence save for the mounting madness of the sirens and the moan of straining motors. Wentworth could see the building of the broadcasting company clearly now—see where the flames spurted like living, sentient things from high windows. A policeman sprang into the street to stop the taxi; all traffic was being turned aside.

"This will do," Wentworth directed quietly. "Pull to the curb, and I will wait."

Useless to drive his way through the encircling lines of the police. The building was doomed. It would be gutted on every floor before those flames were conquered. Could any man live through such an inferno? Wentworth doubted that Kalki had even entered the building. The fire could disrupt the control, and the wires could be tapped elsewhere. But he must wait, to be sure, while police and firemen ringed the building. The danger was that the police might fail to recognize Kalki if he had assumed disguise. The Spider would not fail!

He turned the radio to the police signal band and heard Dane's voice, harsh upon the air. There was weariness in Dane's voice, and a tinging of hopeless fury. Wentworth nodded at the fact that Dane had thrown a police cordon about the Temple of Vishnu. In that way, he could hope to intercept Kalki if the man returned to the building… He could intercept him, but could he hope to take, or hold him captive under the assault of the flames of Vishnu? There was only one answer to that. The police should open fire at sight, and riddle Kalki with the law's lead. Yet they could not. But there was nothing to stop the Spider!

WHEN PRESENTLY it became clear that there was no hope of finding Kalki in the fire district, Wentworth had the taxi carry him toward the temple and there took up his lonely watch. The night dragged out and the altar fire that greeted the dawn sent up its cat-tongue of red atop the temple… and there was no trace of Kalki for all the hundreds of police who kept watch. No trace of Kalki, but in the cold chill hour before the dawn, people began to creep from the dark streets and automobiles began to deliver their cargoes of humanity to the district.

They went timidly, these people, across the wide cobbles of South Street and the mouth of the Temple of Vishnu was open to swallow them! The mandates and the threats of Kalki were bearing fruit!

A fury shook Wentworth at the sight, but he acknowledged that he could not blame the people. They did not know, did not care, if they were being victimized. They sought only safety from the all-devouring flames which had struck tragedy into so many homes within the last forty-eight hours. Freedom of worship, the government granted all people. Kalki might be destroyed, but the temple would continue to draw its thousands, its tens of thousands, so long as the flames of Vishnu remained unexplained, and unconquered.

It was a staggering criminal plan, for Wentworth did not for a moment doubt that this talk of gods and worship was a blind. If all churches became one church, if the people of a whole nation poured through the portals of the temples of Vishnu and lived under the constant threat of the flames, they would pay millions into the coffers of Kalki and the men behind him. Millions on millions of dollars! Yes, it was a treasure that men would kill for, ruthlessly and by the thousand!

At long last, when it became clear that Kalki himself would not appear, Wentworth turned wearily away and dragged his exhausted body, his feverishly wounded leg, through the city streets toward an obscure hotel. One thing he did before he flung himself down to get the rest he must have. He telephoned to a group of private investigators which, at times as Richard Wentworth, he had employed to pursue minor phases of the Spider's work.

"A cash retainer will be sent to you by messenger before noon," he told them, "but I want you to get to work immediately. In California three years ago, a cult leader was arrested on extortion charges. The newspapers will give you his name. Eighteen months ago, there was a similar case against another such man. Get the details of those cases together, and any other similar cases you can find. I will phone for a report and tell you what to do farther. I want descriptions."

And Wentworth bathed his fevered wound and forced his taut body and mind into the blank of sleep....

THE SPIDER slept. He was one man, and human despite the incredible things he accomplished, and he was alone and hunted, with a feverish wound in his thigh. But the priests and the servants of Vishnu, of Kalki, his avatar, were many... and not all of them slept. There were those who had slept during the day so that the work could be carried on. Kalki had pledged a thousand unbelieving souls to Vishnu on this day, and it was a pledge that must be kept, that would be kept....

In the city's tens of thousand homes people were awakening to begin their day of work—the work that must go on though flames danced terribly across the city and struck, and struck again. A man must work if his family is to eat; women must hurry to the offices to earn their quota of the bread of life. The subways will still run, and the stores will open and there will be shoppers. The trucks must carry food to the shops, and all the multiple small jobs of the city must be carried on. They awoke... and prepared for the day.

Those who had not heard the thunder of Kalki's threats over the radio, read them in the shrieking newspapers on the way to work. But those who had not seen the flames of Vishnu—those who had not been touched by their tragedy—read it as a thing apart from themselves as people will. It was a news story, something that had no personal meaning.

"A thousand will be killed each day," they read, and perhaps looked a little anxiously about them. And saw the familiar crowd, the people jammed close together, swaying in the subway aisles, thought drowned in the mechanic hammer and roar of their speed… and were reassured. Like soldiers in the moment of battle, they thought "The other fellow, the other woman, will get it—not me. I feel lucky. Not me…."

They thought like that until the bullet that had their name upon it reached its billet. They had a brief moment then of surprise, of disbelief, before pain and the blackness of death ended all thought. The people in the subways were like that, if they knew fear at all.

The Spider slept… but the priests of Vishnu did not. Times Square's network of underground walkways brought two great subway systems together, sucked in the thousands from Brooklyn, from Queens, from the Bronx and all Manhattan, and spewed them out upon the streets, hurrying throngs on their way to the offices. Individuals with their lone thoughts, their single harassments and dreams.

A girl in rose and blue, ridiculous for an office, but a bright bit of saucy life that drew many eyes. She was early, humming a little tune. Frank would be at the office early, too. Her hand fluttered up to her curled hair. She felt *right* this morning. She felt lucky….

A man in a soiled panama hat, his head pulled down, walking swiftly and frowning through his glasses. Orders falling off, and he had to find a way to pick them up. If he didn't show a profit this month again, there might be changes….

An office clerk paused to eye a newsstand, hurriedly bought a race-track tip-sheet and hurried off, peering hungrily between its bright-inked covers. A two-dollar bet on Limberlegs now, at seven-to-one… They thought of these little personal things, and forgot that Vishnu must have his thousand lives.

The crowd jammed in the exit stairs, moving slowly, ponderously, and more thousands slammed into the station at each roaring crescendo of the trains. A thousand lives? Well, a few more wouldn't matter… and the Spider slept. Did he stir uneasily with the rack of dreams, or thought that would not still in his brain? Or perhaps, it was the pain of his wounded leg.

It was the girl in rose and blue who first knew that Vishnu was claiming his sacrifice. Perhaps it was because her eyes were larger, because they were bright and liquid with excitement. She frowned a little and blinked at a dryness in her eyeballs. Something in her eyes… She reached up a gaily-gloved hand to rub it, but the dryness did not ease. Her eyes watered, and the pain was like the thrust of a knife. She bit her lip, tried to force her way upward through the slow-moving crowd… and couldn't. She fought against that pain, as against an external thing, but a cry was wrung from her….

It was a low, moaning, whimpering cry and she whipped both hands to her face, and ground the palms hard against her eyes. Just afterward, she screamed. There was that tragic spurt of fire that quivered over her eyes, that laced about her fingers, that pushed its tendrils into the softness of her curled hair, and writhed out from beneath her clothing. A few people had turned to stare at her first moan, but not for long. For the flames of Vishnu had begun their work, their eager, corybantic dancing, and one girl's screams did not matter.

She fell, and there were a hundred feet tramping over her

collapsed, flaming body; a hundred and a thousand feet, and she was not alone now, writhing on the steps. There was a man whose glasses were shattered and whose worries were done, and there was a torn tip-sheet on the floor and the clerk writhed nearby—writhed for a while and was still....

ALL THAT gloomy horror beneath the earth was lit by lurid flames, was mad with the screams, and the stampeding panic, with death. Men ran blindly, even before the flames reached them. They struck other men, they trampled women and weaker men; they fought with the craziness of animals, all thought left save preservation.

The flames and the panic killed its scores, killed its hundreds. Those familiar underground tunnels had become a trap, so that men thought for the first time of the thousands of buildings and pavements above them, and the thought was madness... for it closed them in.

The stench of the burning, and the black smoke of the torment was thick in the air... and the trains continued to run, continued to empty their hundreds and their thousands out upon the narrow platforms, until the concrete islands were jammed, until the steps that led upward were blocked with fallen, burning bodies; until, when they stopped, more men fought wildly to get into the cars; until the tracks were jammed with the dying, and no more trains could run.

Kalki had promised a thousand lives to Vishnu, and he kept his promise tenfold in that brief hour when the flames visited Times Square station. The horror of it would live through years of dread, and when the radio yelped with the news of it, when the papers poured upon the streets with the threat and the tragedy of it, the people realized for the first time that this was no longer a matter of "the other fellow." It was something that gnawed in each individual soul, that crept into every quaking home. And that fact had its sure result....

At first, there was only that thin dawn trickle toward the Temple of Vishnu, but by ten o'clock, the streets that led that way were jammed with hurrying, fearful people; with people who stared, haunted by terror, about them. At noon, the width of South Street was jammed from the walls of the temple to the drab walls of the warehouses beyond, and still the people came. The streets that led into it were solid with standing, with pleading people.

Police tried to turn them aside and there was no stopping them, for fear was eating at their vitals, a fear greater than any mere dread of a man with a gun. For they fled from what they could not understand, from flames that struck without any reason, and they were crying out to the one man who could save them from such horror; to the man who had brought it upon them... to Kalki, avatar of Vishnu!

This was at noon... and it was at noon that the Spider dragged himself out from the brief sleep that he had allowed himself, because human flesh could prevail no longer. His wound was better and he stood before a mirror, stripped to the waist, and methodically destroyed the disguise that had turned him into Jenkyns. He was looking at his face, not at his body, which was lean and tanned and hard... and wealed by the white cicatrices of a hundred scars suffered in the battles for mankind.

He had faced death so many times and now once more he was ready to hurl himself, single-handed, into the warfare against Kalki… a warfare in which the police already had failed; the twenty thousand police of New York City had failed. And it was no shame to them, for this was a thing beyond the understanding of man, and there was a terror beyond the reach of the law. But the Spider would not, could not fail… not while he lived.

A brief, cold smile touched the undisguised face of Richard Wentworth, sharpened the thin bridge of the aristocratic nose, turned the kindly mouth ruthless and hard. For, in his sleep, unconsciously, he had formed a plan. And it brought the risk of death, almost the certainty of death, very close. Only the Spider could not even afford to die!

Kalki was in hiding, and the police would try to hound him, but the Spider had an approach of which they knew nothing. The priests of Vishnu knew that an old street musician had entered their temple and, in the cell to which he had been assigned, the seal of the Spider had been affixed! And that same seal had desecrated their shrine of the avatars! Wentworth thought that the vengeful priests and their criminal cohorts would be looking for the Spider, and they would seek him in the guise of the aged musician! It was the Spider's intention that they should find him!

Under the skillful touch of his hands, employing some of the few articles preserved from the destruction of that secret room in Nita's apartment, the skin of his face drew taut and sallow across the strong, shapely bones of his face. He made a beak of his thin-bridged aristocratic nose. A few touches more and he could convert this countenance of his into the ominous face of the Spider, but for the present it was enough that he should become the musician.

He left off the heavy brows of the Spider, merely roughening his own; and the lank long hair of the Spider's wig was carefully brushed and shaped into the flowing locks of the musician. And his mouth remained kind. The clothes of Jenkyns would do well enough, with the addition of a shoe string tie.

Now Wentworth was ready. First to the safety-deposit box which he held in the name of the street musician, Casimir Belotti, to send money to the detective agency, and then… and then to the barren lodgings of Casimir Belotti to await the killers of Kalki!

The time had come….

IT WAS in the lobby that Wentworth first heard the rumors of the vast throngs flocking toward the temple of Kalki. The radio blared out the announcements of a newscaster; the slaughter of the subway, the rush of thousands to the temple, were being told in a variety of infinite detail.

The anger and the sense of futility that had hounded him since first he had battled with Kalki returned in overwhelming force, and Wentworth moved heavily into the street. People scurried past him on the walks, and cars racketed impatiently at the corners. The stream of human beings was flowing in only one direction… toward the Temple of Vishnu.

For a long minute, Wentworth stood on the pavement and watched the white-faced throngs scuttle past, with fright on their white faces. The temptation was strong upon Wentworth to join the migration so that once more he might enter the temple and seek Kalki. However, he was sure it would prove futile. Kalki would not hide himself so obviously. No, it was much surer to return to his own habitat as Casimir Belotti and invite the killers to come for him! That way he was more certain of challenge, more likely to come to grips with the monster behind these atrocities! Nor did he want to turn aside the people from their rush to the comparative safety of the temple. For them, there should be no danger of the flames....

Wentworth sent the money to the detective agency and thereafter went to the cheap lodgings of Casimir Belotti... and waited. The long hours of the day dragged past, and there came no interruption of his quiet. Only by a violent exertion of his will was he able to remain inactive there, though reason told him it was the best move.

Kalki had claimed his victims for the day and, before another dawn, the killers might come for the Spider! If they had not acted by the time the night had waned, he would try another method. Only twice during the long day did Wentworth leave his quarters—once to eat, and once to phone the detectives. They gave him the names of a half dozen men accused of making a racket of religion and physical descriptions of them, and none of them had the fierce red mane of Kalki. But there *was* one with a hideous scar across his cheek.

"Dickinson is the only one I'm interested in," Wentworth told them over the phone, naming the man with the scar. "See what you can do about locating his present whereabouts. There will be a bonus for fast work."

Then he went back to wait and watch, and to steel his soul to patience while the city's thousands poured into the temple of Vishnu and worshiped before the altar of flame. Toward the hour of dawn, he, himself, made the pilgrimage—but was stopped by the shuffling throngs which still choked the streets and hour by hour shambled forward to file past the altar, to gain what they hoped was immunity against the flames which could burst from a man's eyes and destroy all his body... and which came from no human being knew where—unless from hostile gods as Kalki declared. For hours then, Wentworth combed the underworld, seeking some hint of where Kalki next would strike. But he could find no clue.

There was a gauntness about Wentworth's face when, late in the afternoon, he limped back toward the lodging house. He would give Kalki's agents one more chance to attack him here, and then... and then he would carry the battle to the temple itself! From the water, he could reach the building and clamber to the roof entrance of those secret passages. It would increase his danger a hundred-fold and reduce almost to nil his chances of surviving the attack to locate and slay Kalki; to ferret out finally the secret of the flames of Vishnu.

And so Wentworth delayed... Not that he feared death, or that he hesitated to run the risk of torture and destruction. Too many times in the swift years, he had been face to face with the Grim Specter to fear him now. But if he died, who would save the thousands of the city from this fearful parasite that had fastened itself upon them?

PAINFULLY, WENTWORTH turned into the dingy

doorway of his lodging house and made his way up the stairs. Footsteps were ascending ahead of him, he realized suddenly. He checked to listen acutely but shook his head. It was only the landlady, going to clean up her lodgers' rooms. Hers was a night-working, day-sleeping clientele and she would be just beginning her work now. Wentworth climbed more rapidly, reached the head of the second-floor steps as the woman bent to thrust a key into the lock of his door.

"It isn't fastened, Mrs. Hilly," he said gently.

Mrs. Hilly straightened with a jerk, her red face stiffening. "Oh, I didn't hear you, Mr. Belotti, until you spoke. All this stuff that's happening gives anybody a case of nerves, it does. Do you want I should wait to clean up your room?"

Wentworth lifted his shoulders, "There is no need to wait." He thrust open the door and the woman heaved her heavy body through the doorway, began to slap the pillows on the bed.

"Enough to drive anybody crazy, thinking about what's happened," Mrs. Hilly rambled on garrulously. "As if anybody would leave the true church on that heathen's say-so! Father Caddis says the man is a faker."

Wentworth crossed to the window and stood staring out at the westering sun. A faker Kalki might be, but there was nothing faked about the flames of Vishnu, except their origin. They were very real and their torment was a deadly thing.

Wentworth's arms tautened with the readiness for battle. He had waited too long already though, God knew, his invasion of the temple gave small promise of success. He turned abruptly aside from the window. Now was the time to strike—now before a new flood of horror was released, and… He cut off short, staring at Mrs. Hilly. She was rubbing her eyes.

"I declare," she said irritably, "I don't know where all this dust comes from. Seems like the air is full of it… Holy Mary, how it hurts!"

Wentworth let out a strangled shout of horror as he realized the truth. The killers of Kalki had come in his absence, and… He cut off the thought, leaping toward a pitcher of water on a washstand against the wall. Mrs. Hilly was grinding the heels of her hands into her eyes.

"Quickly!" he snapped. "Take your hands down!"

Mrs. Hilly uttered a choked cry. "Oh, God, it *hurts!* It…."

With a savage oath, Wentworth jerked at her hands and flung the contents of the pitcher squarely into Mrs. Hilly's eyes! She staggered backward, staring at him incredulously, and the side of the bed caught her behind the knees, spilled her upon it. The shaft of sunlight, slanting through the window, showed a myriad dust motes dancing in the air, billowing up under the impact of her fall and Wentworth's eyes narrowed at the sight, even as he sprang into action.

"Quickly!" he cried. "Out of here! It's deadly! It's the flames of Vishnu!"

He caught Mrs. Hilly by her thick wrists, jerked her from the bed and propelled her toward the door. He closed his eyes with fierce strength, shouting at the woman to do the same. There was a convulsive resistance in her body, a jerking and trembling as if she fought to remain in the room. Her scream came out hoarsely, terribly and, suddenly, Wentworth knew the searing touch of flame upon his hands! He whipped them free as he jerked the door shut behind him, and his eyes flew wide. Little runlets of liquid flame were dripping down the back of Mrs. Hilly's neck!

Violently, Wentworth whipped off his coat and flung it about her, thrust her to the floor while her arms flailed and her whole body fought wildly against his efforts. And it was in vain. For a moment, he had thought the flames of Vishnu were beaten, and then they were everywhere. They lanced out through the scorching material of his coat; they billowed out beneath the doomed woman's skirts and consumed them in a flash; they leaped from the tips of her threshing hands.

And still Wentworth fought on, trying to save her, trying to smother the flames that would not be blotted out. He ignored the scorching of his hands, but the strength of the woman's agony was too much for even the Spider's whipcord strength. She jerked free of his grip, plunged down the stairs with the streamers of flame standing out straight behind her. She screamed hoarsely, without words, like a tortured animal. Doors flicked open along the halls, slammed again at the sight of that horror. ON THE second floor, Wentworth stood motionless and there was a heat in his veins that had nothing to do with flame. He was the cause of this woman's death, for the trap of Kalki had been set for him, and no other! He should have guessed what form their attempt would take and forbidden the woman to enter his room. Damn it, he could not understand this! The men must have known that he had been in the temple, and had gained a certain immunity to the death flames! Perhaps that immunity wore off, had to be renewed? Yes, that must be it, and they had figured that the concentration of the substance that brought it about, in this closed room, would eliminate the Spider!

Wentworth's lips parted in a grimace of hatred and determination. This once they had overreached themselves. They had revealed to him that a fine dust, spread in the air, was responsible for the flames. In that room, he could trap some of the powder, analyze it, and... He spun back toward the room and a curse leaped from his tightened throat! Beneath the door, tongues of flame were licking out! Too late! He had delayed too long!

Wentworth swung about and went down the steps in long bounds. They had made their attack upon him, and they had failed... they had killed this poor, struggling woman in his place. He would see to it that they had no chance to fail again! His hands brushed lightly at his sides, felt the weight of his automatic, and the other bulges which marked the leather pouch girdle about his waist. He had weapons there that could destroy the entire temple of Vishnu! He had discarded most of the tools he usually carried. In their places were tube after tube of the two liquids which, mixed together, produced the terrifically powerful explosive that he had used with such devastating effect upon his steel-lined secret room!

Wentworth was conscious only dimly of the voices of people about him as he hurried toward the street. But their words registered on his brain, to come clearly to him presently as he hurried forth to battle. "She said it was a fake," one man had whispered. "And she's dead! That settles it... I'm going to the temple!"

To the temple! All the city would be pouring toward the temple soon. One more such slaughter as had taken place in the subway. Kalki would soon become too powerful to destroy! Under the fear of the flame, the very people he victimized would fight the vengeance of the Spider, and of the law! Once Wentworth checked in his swift progress to turn in a fire alarm, then he hurried on to a telephone booth. He would need allies for his frontal attack upon Kalki... Ram Singh and Jackson! God knew three men would be none too many for the thing that he planned!

His call to Nita's home went through swiftly, but it was the aged, grave voice of Jenkyns that answered him.

"Oh, Master Richie!" he cried, "if only you had called yesterday! Miss Nita and Ram Singh and Jackson have gone, sir!"

"Gone where?" Wentworth felt the tightening of his chest.

"To the temple, sir! Oh, to the temple!" Jenkyns rushed on. "I tried to stop them, sir, but Miss Nita said it was where you would be, and she must be there to help you. She said the temple would need priestesses, and she... Ram Singh and Jackson followed her against her orders, but they can't stop her, sir. That's twenty-four hours ago, and I haven't heard from them since! If there's anything...."

"Just stay there," Wentworth's voice had an ominous quiet. "I will call you again when I can. You must relay messages."

"Wait, Master Richie!" Jenkyns gasped. "The other phone, the private phone is ringing, and it may be...."

"Answer it, man!"

Wentworth beat his fist softly against the wall of the booth while long seconds dragged past and he heard muted sounds his straining ears could not interpret. Then, suddenly, Jenkyns was stammering excitedly over the wire again.

"Oh, sir," he cried. "It's… It's Miss Nita. It's desperate, most desperate, and she…."

"Steady, Jenkyns," Wentworth said quietly. "Take both phones and plug them into the same socket and let me talk directly to Miss Nita."

"But, sir—"

JENKYNS HAD to be told twice and then Wentworth heard explosive clicks and, abruptly, Nita's hurried voice was in his ear. "Thank God, I've reached you, Dick," she said, and it was in a frantic whisper that she spoke. "Tomorrow, Kalki is going to herd all the converts together and they will pull the cart of the Juggernaut through the streets of the city. Every church they pass will be burned with everyone in it. You've got to warn them."

Wentworth spoke quietly, while his heart raced with the direful news, "Good work, Nita! Leave the temple at once! I'm going to destroy it!"

"I can't Dick," Nita whispered, "and you can't destroy the temple! There must be fully ten thousand people in it at this moment! There are never less than that. They come all the time, and… Oh, good-by, Dick!"

Her voice rose with anxiety and Wentworth called sharply to her. Over the wire, he heard a man's deep voice echo on a note of harsh anger just before the line was disconnected—and he knew that voice… he knew it terribly! It was the voice of Kalki, avatar of Vishnu!

Wentworth hung up the receiver and stared through an agonized moment, blindly, at the wall. God! Nita had been caught in the act of revealing Kalki's secrets! Ten thousand innocents thronged the temple to block any move that the Spider might make, and tomorrow... tomorrow the cart of the Juggernaut would carry death and the destruction of the flames of Vishnu throughout the city!

Wentworth ripped out a savage oath. His own course was clear! He must find Commissioner Sanford Dane and force him, somehow, to prevent the churches from opening tomorrow! Only when he had done that did he dare risk his life to save Nita, to destroy Kalki. Otherwise, the churches would not be warned. Damn Sanford Dane for a stubborn fool! It was not enough that he telephone the man. He must go to him, hammer belief into Dane's obstinate brain. And meanwhile, God alone knew what would happen to Nita!

Wentworth tore open the door of the booth—and pulled up to a sharp halt! The proprietor of the drugstore, from which he had phoned, was sprawled senseless on the floor behind his counter! There were four men ringed about the entrance of the booth. Three of them held ready revolvers and the fourth pointed the deadly muzzle of a machine-gun at the Spider's body!

"You will come with us!" said the machine-gunner softly. "You will come to us for judgment before the throne of Vishnu! Or you can take your judgment here and now, Spider... *a stream of lead in the guts!*"

CHAPTER 8
SACRIFICE OF VISHNU

WENTWORTH'S HANDS were empty of weapons and he knew that before even his super-trained hands could draw a gun, he would be pierced a dozen times by deadly lead. Yet such was the drive of his desperation that he swayed forward on the point of empty-handed attack upon the gunmen of Vishnu! It took a violent exertion of will to relax the quiver of his fighting muscles. This was not the moment for the Spider to force the issue!

A few minutes before, Wentworth had been gambling his life to achieve this same captivity at the hands of Kalki's man, risking everything to confront Kalki. Now that his plan had succeeded, he knew it would be fatal... fatal to the thousands of innocents threatened by the slaughter of Vishnu upon the morrow! But there was no escape; he was helpless. Wentworth smothered a groan of despair in his soul, but on his face was a quiet smile. He nodded to the gunmen who ringed him in.

"Gentlemen," he said softly, "it seems you have the advantage!"

The machine-gunner twisted his thin ascetic's face into a scowl. "Exactly," he said harshly, "and we shall keep it!"

At his nod, one of the other gunmen circled Wentworth and his rapid search revealed not only the Spider's automatic but the girdle of invaluable tools about his waist! For a frantic moment, as the man stripped off the girdle, Wentworth was on the point of hurling himself upon the searcher, attempting to interpose the man's body between himself and the machine-gun.

Without those tools, his chances of converting this tragic defeat into victory were reduced a thousand-fold! The urge to action trembled through his body; his brain behind the quiet masking smile was on fire with half-formed plans. The machine-gun checkmated them all. Even if he got the gunner between himself and that hose of death, it would accomplish nothing. Machine-gun lead, six hundred a minute, would claw its fierce way completely through such a human shield in the course of split-seconds and... the Spider would die! No, no, the Spider could not afford to risk his life. It was not his to risk so madly when thousands of human souls depended upon his survival! The Spider... submitted.

Despair stalked with Wentworth as he marched between two guards toward the car at the curb, the machine-gun grinding in his spine. He had been stripped of his last tool and weapon. Captive of Kalki, fore-doomed by the judgment of Vishnu... yet somehow he must break through this circle of death to save the people, to destroy the monster who threatened them. Somehow... Crazy laughter swelled in his throat and the men stared at him curiously, warily.

Nothing interrupted their swift trip to the Temple of Vishnu. The car rolled into a warehouse across the street from the temple and it was through underground tunnels that he was conducted into the building itself. Overhead he could hear the massed voices of thousands of citizens chanting out the slow, heavy hymns of Vishnu and his soul writhed at his helplessness. Since he had been brought to the temple itself, obviously Kalki was here… and Nita! God in heaven, what was happening to her now, caught in the act of betrayal!

No word was spoken and the silent beat of his captors' feet was the only accompaniment of their passage through half-darkness, and always men's hands were hard upon his arms and always the deadly snout of that machine-gun tortured his back. When he came to a halt finally, it was before the uncurtained entrance of a priest's cell and, from it, came the wry, monkey-faced man in his golden robe, his withered stick of an arm lifted in benediction. The hatred in his beady eyes was like a touch of flame.

"Ah, the Spider," he said softly. "Bring him this way!"

ONCE MORE the march through the tunnels resumed, but now the way led downward and dampness and cold pressed in upon Wentworth. He could feel it in his wounded leg. Moisture condensed on the stone walls. The priest's bare feet made small whispering sounds, like the dragging of a snake's scales over rock, and he ducked presently through a dark arch and a torch began to lift its red, smoky flare.

From some recess of his robes, he drew a ring of keys and it was then that Wentworth saw what was in store for him. In an instant, men's hands were ripping off his clothing, tore off even his shoes! He was thrown violently against the wall. Its cold ran bitterly through his body, but there was no time to strike out. Men pinned his arms against the stone and steel manacles, riveted there, snapped home about his wrists. There was a collar for his throat, and another to clamp his waist hard against the wall!

Fury swelled Wentworth's throat, but he compelled himself to remain calm. Four locked collars of steel fastened him stiffly against the wall, strained so high that his toes could barely reach the floor. Helpless, completely helpless… and he might be left here for hours, might be left so until the cart of the Juggernaut had carried its destruction through the city streets.

Wentworth twisted his neck inside the collar that half-strangled him, and his voice came out hoarsely as he stared down at the gunmen and the bitter-faced priest of Vishnu, whose mouth was like a puckered scar.

"There's some mistake," Wentworth said slowly, "you haven't put anything about my ankles."

No one answered him and the eyes of the men glowed with fanatic fires. The priest licked his scarlike lips. "You may go," he said softly to the others. "Kalki shall know of your achievement and Vishnu will reward you. Go… I will keep the guard!"

"Yes, Dangri!" murmured the machine-gunner. There was a thin, anticipatory smile on his lips as he withdrew. The priest called Dangri did not even look toward them. He kept his beady eyes upon Wentworth and his hand was slipping inside his silken robe. It came out slowly… with a knife!

"There is something in what you say," Dangri murmured. "Your feet do constitute a menace!" He moved forward warily!

Because of the strain of the binding collars, Wentworth could see the priest only by twisting his head sideways and staring down out of the corners of his eyes. He made hard work of breathing, and his arms were already aching with the stretched tension of his manacles. And the priest was gliding toward him, with the knife poised point forward. The torchlight gleamed upon its razor edge, staining it as red as if already it had eaten into Wentworth's flesh.

"Hamstrung," Dangri whispered. "A simple process. Just a matter of sliding the knife across the back of the ankle, or the back of the knees… and your feet cease to be a menace. As a matter of fact, they cease to be of any value to you. But that won't matter, eh, Spider? Those who are sacrificed to Vishnu never again have need to walk!"

Wentworth's voice came out in a hoarse whimper. "For God's sake, Dangri, loosen this collar about my throat. I'm strangling!" He writhed a little against the grip of his steel collars and his feet drummed vainly against the wall.

Dangri… giggled. He pricked Wentworth's left ankle with the knife point and Wentworth whipped his feet aside, frantically, kept them lifted high to the side. Dangri reached out for them with the knife and Wentworth jerked them in the opposite direction. His breast was panting and the veins of his throat were swollen. His face was a mask of terror and despair, but behind that mask his keen brain was at work, furiously.

His fright was a deliberate pretense, but the helplessness was no disguise. He had no weapon save his feet. There was a chance, a thread of a chance that he might use them successfully, but he would need to draw Dangri into exactly the right position. Even so, it was much more likely that he would take that foot-long knife through his stomach! There was no other way.

CALMLY, WENTWORTH contemplated the possibility of being hamstrung. If he permitted Dangri to succeed in that, would he be left alone then? Would he have more chance of getting free and destroying Kalki and this vile temple? Incredible that even a man of Wentworth's sacrificial temperament could calmly consider such a thing... and yet he did. It was not beyond the will of this Master of Men to allow himself to be crippled if, by that means, he could succeed in saving the people!

Dangri was growing exasperated with Wentworth's agile whipping aside of his legs. He poised the knife for a determined thrust at those knees... and he came forward to do it... within a yard of the wall to which Wentworth was chained! Once more, the Spider dodged. He spread his legs, one as far to the left as possible, the other as far to the right while he tautened his muscles against the collars for purchase. Dangri laughed, poised the knife again... and Wentworth struck!

It was a mad thing he tried, but there was no other way. His legs whipped forward and his heels hooked behind the loins of Dangri, tightened in a scissor hold that made the muscles leap out in copper bands upon his thighs! But he could not hold that. It left Dangri's arms free and, after the first moment of shock, that knife would be seeking Wentworth's vitals!

Wentworth dragged the man close to the wall and, with a violent effort, flung him flat on his back upon the stone floor! Wentworth's breath strangled against the confining collar. The rough edge of it bit into his throat as he twisted his head in a frantic effort to see. Now was the acute moment. If he could just manage....

His left foot groped along the man's out-thrown knife arm in a swift, gliding movement, pinned the knife-wrist to the floor.

His right foot found and clamped down upon Dangri's throat! And Wentworth threw all his suspended weight—all the power of his thigh muscle upon that downward pressure—grinding Dangri's neck against the stone floor! There would not be time to strangle the man. He would cross his left hand over to that knife. Wentworth could no longer see him. Straining downward in his collar, the Spider's head was twisted so that he stared straight upward at the ceiling. He was strangling himself!

His heel sought for the windpipe. He could feel Dangri writhing like a pinioned snake. A foot reached up and struck Wentworth in the body and torture raked its claws through his vitals. But he was sure of his position now.

With the convulsive speed of a tiger's spring, Wentworth lifted his right foot and drove it downward again! The frenzy of movement afterward jerked Dangri free of Wentworth's awkward grip. There was a rattling awful sound of clogged breath and the drumming of bare heels upon the floor. Through a long moment, the sound continued and, afterward, there was silence. Wentworth hung in his chains and sucked air deeply into his lungs. He knew that he had struck true. His heel had crushed the man's windpipe!

But, God, there was no time to waste! At any moment, one of those men might return, or Kalki himself might inquire into the new captive his men had taken.

Wentworth twisted about to peer toward the limp and motionless body of Dangri. The most difficult part of his task remained. Somehow, with his feet, he had to locate the keys on Dangri's body; he must make sure of his hold upon them so there would be no danger of their falling beyond his reach and then… and then he must lift a foot until those keys reached his right hand. He must contrive to figure out which was the right key, twist his wrist until it reached into the keyhole and unsnap the manacle that held it. After that, the rest would be simple. *After that!* Wentworth began groping with his feet….

During that slow and difficult task, Wentworth lost all conception of the lapse of time. Before he finally succeeded in finding the keys and getting a grip on them with his toes, the torch burned out and flickered into darkness, leaving a blackness that was absolute as death. Through that he had to grope his foot upward to meet his hand… and more time dragged past in futile effort.

Under the torment of the strangling, confining collars, Wentworth's mind went blank of all save that single thing and when, at long last, he completed his release, he leaned weakly against the wall and could not think at all.

THEN A frenzy fell upon him… Time had passed. It might already be the hour when the cart of Juggernaut set forth upon the city streets. Certainly, it could not be long before the continued absence of Dangri was investigated. Wentworth stooped over the stiffened body of the man and wrenched off the robes, draped them over his own shoulders.

He lifted Dangri and clamped the collar close about his twisted neck. There was time for no more, and rigor mortis had gripped the body in its iron mold. In the dark, Wentworth fumbled with the body, testing the completeness of the onset of the stiffening of death. The jaw and shoulders were rigid as iron, but there was some flexibility left in the limbs. Between four and six hours then... God, what could have happened in that time!

Wentworth was made forcibly aware of the fatigue of his body when he reeled out into the corridor. His legs would scarcely support him, and all his body felt bone-weary. He paused, bracing an arm against the dank wall, sucked in long steadying breaths. He had need to think. Kalki had been in this temple several hours before, and Nita... God alone knew what had happened to her after Kalki's discovery that she was a spy! But if she still... lived!

Wentworth rested his forehead against the coldness of the wall and the touch was grateful to the feverishness that was shaking him. Nita... That was a thing he could not think of, yet he must! If she still lived, she offered his best chance of ferreting out, not only the secrets of this temple, but also of locating Kalki himself! Well, if she were within his hearing, he could find her at once! He need only to whistle, to hum a tune that she would recognize, the air of the serenade he had played to her so often upon his violin. A love song... and, dear God, she might be... might be *dead!*

Wentworth stole a short way along the corridor and moistened his lips to whistle, but he could make no sound with his suddenly parched lips. His voice when he drove it to phrase a note, was cracked and harsh, but he had no mercy for himself. He brought out the tune softly, sent it gently along the tunnel beneath the Temple of Vishnu.

"In the gloaming, oh my darling, when the lights are dim and low," he sang softly.

134

Death attended him while he sang, he knew. Any priest of Vishnu who heard him would sound the alarm, but he was in unknown ways and his voice must guide him… even though it led him to death! The close walls beat back the muted tones of his voice, and brought no other answer so that the song choked and died in his throat. His mind glanced away from the thought of Nita, and he pressed on and, presently tried again.

> *"Will you think of me, and love me,*
> *As you did once long ago?"*

And still there was no answer save the dying, whispering echo of his own voice sobbing off through the dark tunnels, the faint rustle of his silken robe and the sibilance of his naked feet upon the floor.

Distantly, there was a dim sound as if men, a large body of men, were walking, but even as he caught it, the murmur of it died away. They had, perhaps, taken another turning in this blind network of tunnels. For a hundred, two hundred feet, Wentworth crept silently on through the darkness. This was madness! Singing love songs in the darkness to a sweetheart who might be… who might never hear him again. He was singing against hope, against all reason and belief… and he could not stop. It was as if, once he stopped, there was no longer any hope of finding Nita safe.

He found a place where tunnels branched and stood there, irresolute. He started a phrase of music, and his throat closed. No, it was hopeless. Give it up… He sang again. He finished the line and his voice died. He bowed his face into his hands.

He was not listening. He took long, slow steps into the darkness… and stopped!

HE HEARD… No, it couldn't be. It was the echo of his own voice, of his own hopes. He wanted so desperately to hear an answer, that he had conjured it out of the thin air. No, no, he was wrong. It couldn't be an echo. It was the next phrase, an answer to his own. *It was Nita!* She sang the phrase through and Wentworth, rock still, listened and then answered—heard the sweet softness of her voice reply again.

"Nita!" It was a shout, a whisper. He plunged blindly along the tunnel. He struck the wall and caromed against the opposite side. He forced himself to stand still, listening, waiting. This time, the whisper was almost at his elbow and he whirled that way, calling her name softly. A sob answered him and he went leaping blindly, arms outstretched… and found chains. Nita's soft, sweet body was chained to the cold, rocky wall as he himself had been. He clasped her to him, felt the warmth of her lips against his cheek and then… he stiffened, listening.

The echo of a shout of alarm ran along the corridor!

"Oh, Dick," Nita gasped, "Oh, Dick…" She drew in a quivering breath and when she spoke again, it was in a rapid, emotionless tone. "You can't get me free, and I have information. Listen! The flames of Vishnu are spread by a dust released into the air. It has an affinity for salt—the salty fluids of the body, tears, perspiration. I got these things from Kalki. He was… attracted by me. Wanted me to become his *sakti,* his goddess-wife, Lakshmi… A chemical dust is released throughout this building. Air conditioning. It has the effect of neutralizing the salty fluids of the body so that there is nothing to ignite the flame dust. You had my warning. Kalki heard, and… Dick, you have a key!"

Wentworth said, softly, "I'm not sure one will fit. I took them from the man who had fastened me up like this. Dangri."

"That snake!" Nita cried. "He fastened me up, too. He has a knife…."

Wentworth laughed, harshly. "I have it now! The key fits!"

The shouts were louder, multiplied in the halls. There was the soft thud of running feet. Nita's freed hand clung to his shoulder, and there was a quiet confidence in the touch, in her voice that sent new life thrilling through all Wentworth's body.

"What shall we do now?" she asked gently.

Wentworth's arm was fiercely about her, and his hand clutched the hilt of his knife as he faced toward the door. He could feel the opening like a weakness in a shield. Through that, danger would come.

"We go to the air-conditioning machine," he said grimly, "and see what can be done about this antidote. You wouldn't know, would you, Nita, if there are supplies of salt in the building?"

Nita's hand tightened on his arm. "There is salt. Kalki uses it on his victims when he wants to make sure they will burn. False priests. He calls it the Holy Water of Father Ganges. If they catch fire afterward, they are guilty. And he makes sure they will by pouring salt into the water!"

Wentworth's sharp laughter was muted. "Good! Lead me to that, and then to the air conditioner… and we will try turning the tables on these priests of Vishnu when they set out tomorrow to burn the churches!"

137

Nita said softly, "It is today, Dick. It lacks only an hour of dawn."

EVEN THE shortness of the time did not daunt Wentworth's spirit now. In freeing Nita, he felt that he had struck a mortal blow at Kalki. If he could free Nita in the heart of the stronghold, then what could he not accomplish? He urged Nita toward the corridor, and the echo of shouts and running was continuous. There was a loud, harsh shout and he caught the echoing name of Dangri. So they had found where the Spider had struck!

"It is this way, I think," Nita whispered, and her hand tugged at the taut muscles of his arm.

As they moved off down the corridor, the tumult faded out behind them. Evidently, it had not occurred to the priests of Vishnu that escaping prisoners would seek to burrow deeper into the fetid tunnels beneath the temple. Yet the danger remained; the thought of those lean fanatics, seeking with their hungry knives poised, was a red spot in Wentworth's brain. Ultimately, he must fight his way through them, or remain hidden here. No, that was unthinkable. When the spreaders of death went forth, the Spider would follow to harry and to slay; to wipe out this threat to the people.

It was the memory of those scores of hunting priests that turned Wentworth's decision when finally Nita had led him to where the sound of the whirring machinery of the air conditioner made further guidance unnecessary. There was a man on guard at the door, dimly visible in the rays that filtered out from within and Wentworth reversed his knife in his hand, hurled it with a swift, overhand sweep of his arm. The hilt thudded into the guard's temple and he pitched sideways.

In two long bounds, Wentworth was upon the man, dragging him into the machinery room. A swift survey showed him what he had come to learn. A hopper filled with a delicately spun powder fed into the conditioner slowly, and this was swept through conduits to every corner of the temple. This was what had made him and the police who had entered the building immune to the later outbreaks of the flames of Vishnu. It was what Kalki would count on to protect his men when the cart of the Juggernaut rolled!

Wentworth sprang at the machine and with a quick jerk wedged the mouth of the hopper so that the immunizing powder no longer would circulate. Then he whirled to the supply room which fortunately adjoined it. There were huge bags of salt and, looking at them, Wentworth laughed harshly. It was a thing that could work two ways, this air-conditioning system of Kalki. It could spread death as well as immunity! Wentworth bent his back and, at a staggering run, carried a bag of salt to the air conditioner, poured it into the circulating duct; ran back without halting to the supply room. Nita bent to lash and gag the guard whom Wentworth had overpowered.

The exertion of the work brought the perspiration out over Wentworth's body and he felt the sting of the salt he was spilling. A frown dented his forehead. If salt was the touch-off for the flame-dust of Vishnu, he was badly exposed. Kalki would have only to puff a handful of the stuff toward him… Wentworth realized that he had no intention of leaving the temple until he had settled with Kalki! But he could not ask Nita to share the risk of sudden death, would not want her to. On the other hand, now that she was reunited with him, it would be impossible to drive her from his side… unless duty called!

Wentworth dumped the last bag of salt and straightened, breathing deeply from his exertions. But he could not rest. He snatched up one of the bags and filled it from the hopper, beckoned Nita to him.

"Dust yourself thoroughly with this anti-flame powder," he told her quietly. "Then I have a task for you!"

Nita's violet eyes tightened and the line of her round chin became more prominent. "I'm not leaving you here, Dick!" she said firmly.

Wentworth smiled and his hands rested lightly on her shoulders. "I'll be close behind you," he said, "but this is something that must be done. I want you to get to that phone again and call Bishop Harrington. Tell him to request for tomorrow a prayer meeting, and have his congregation call on heaven to… destroy Kalki!"

Nita frowned. "I don't understand," she said. "Why is that necessary?"

Wentworth shook his head. "Don't you see? Kalki has a great hold upon the superstitions of the people. Unless there seems to be something supernatural about his destruction, the people still will not be free of his hold upon them! You will tell Bishop Harrington that the Spider guarantees his safety, and the safety of his congregation!"

Nita drew in a quick breath and her eyes were soft. "Oh, Dick, can you do that?" she whispered. "If you can…."

Wentworth said quietly, "I can, dear, if you'll make this phone call… and afterward take a bag of the immunity powder to Bishop Harrington. I chose him because his is the only church in the city that has a similar air conditioner to this. If he empties this container of powder into his air conditioner… You see, dear, it wasn't just an excuse to get rid of you!"

Nita smiled, and there was no humor in the expression. "No, Dick," she said quietly. "I will get through to the phone. Afterward, I will try to get this bag of the powder to Bishop Harrington. I don't think I can manage more than about forty pounds, but I imagine that will be enough."

"Quite enough," Wentworth agreed.

For a long moment, they stood face-to-face in the room where the machinery gave forth its monotonous hum, where the echoes of the chase through the corridors began to come faintly. Abruptly, Nita flung herself into Wentworth's arms.

"Oh, Dick," she gasped. "How long must this go on? How long must you hide from the police… and from me? I know you do it to spare me, but was it kind to play at being Jenkyns and never… never let me know? Oh, Dick, I…."

Wentworth's arms were fierce about her and his face was turned upward in a dumb pain. He could have no words for Nita, and she knew there was no answer to her plea. As long as the police hounded him for murder, he must remain in hiding; as long as he was in peril of his life from any enemy, he must stay away from Nita. He would save her what he could, though

141

she would persist in throwing herself into his battles. If ever the underworld were finally quieted… Wentworth choked down the self-mockery of his laughter. But that would never come!

"Go now, dear," he said softly. "I have one more errand to perform here, and then…."

"Oh, come with me!" Nita cried. "You can never find your way to Kalki through this maze! In a few hours, he will go upon the streets upon the cart of the Juggernaut and you can find him without fail. There, too, you will have a chance to… to win and survive."

Wentworth set her from him. "Go now, dear," he repeated.

Nita's head bowed and, without more words, she picked up the heavy bag of the immunity dust and slung it across her shoulder. Only at the door she paused again and her faint smile was a plea… a plea that Wentworth had to ignore for her own sake, and for the sake of the people he would serve. He smiled back at her, then turned to the man on the floor. He was conscious now, and he must be placed where he could not tell what had happened here in the machinery chamber. This was a secret Kalki must not penetrate until too late to save his priests and himself.

RAPIDLY, WENTWORTH stripped the priest of his clothing and put them on himself, thrust the man away in the supply room and took his post at the outer door of the chamber where the machinery whirred and whined, pumping death through the temple of Vishnu! This was the only way to make sure that the change was not discovered. To play, himself, the guard of the machinery!

Nita had vanished when he braced his shoulders against the corridor wall outside and presently priests came racing toward him. But he answered their rapid questions shortly and kept his face in shadows—and they raced on. Their shouts and running faded into the darkness and afterward time passed slowly. How much time had passed since he had freed Nita? How long before the cart of the Juggernaut began its lethal passage through the city streets? Surely, not much longer. Before that time, the Spider must find Kalki!

Wentworth knew a calm sureness after his days and hours of despair. He would find Kalki—and when he did, Kalki should die! Even if he failed, even if he died in the attempt, he had set in operation the machinery of eventual retribution. By this time, every priest in the temple, the temple itself, must be thoroughly dusted with salt. The release of the flame powder, whether here or in the streets, would doom them swiftly. Bishop Harrington would call his prayer meeting and, with the help of the dust Nita would carry him, could immunize his congregation and church. Yes, victory was within the Spider's grasp. Victory, and salvation for the people.

What was that?

Wentworth's thoughts broke off short at the harrowing sound that wailed through the corridor, rose, died—shrieked out terribly again. Someone was being tortured! Wentworth shifted his position against the wall and found his hand on the hilt of the knife at his belt. The sound came again, and now he realized there was not one, but many voices united in that cry of agony... the voices of women!

Wentworth swayed out from the wall, and took a slow stride toward the sound. Abruptly, he was running with long, easy bounds and the knife swung free in his hand! Never could the Spider permit wanton torture... but there was an added thought which lent spurs to his running. Where there was torture, he would find Kalki also.

The rise and fall of those awful cries guided Wentworth like a magnet and his pace quickened. He came to an intersection of corridors and swung sharply to the right as the cries came more loudly to his ears. Fury goaded him, and the set of his jaw was fierce. Abruptly, he checked.

Ahead of him, a curtain had been swept aside and he was staring into the leveled and ready muzzle of a machine-gun! He swung about, and now there was a solid rank of priests behind him. They carried guns and knives. Only then did Wentworth realize how neatly he had been trapped. Kalki had found him, as Wentworth had found Nita. He had known that the Spider could never remain idle when human beings were being tortured and, since he could not find the Spider, he had forced Wentworth to betray himself!

"Bring him in," Kalki's deep voice rumbled from the chamber behind the machine-gunner. "Bring him in to be judged before the throne of Vishnu!"

For a mad moment, Wentworth poised on the brink of battle. That machine-gunner dared not loose a blast lest he slaughter the priests behind Wentworth. But he could not be sure the man cared about that, or that the priests themselves cared! Their lives were forfeit before Vishnu and there would be heavenly rewards for martyrdom.

Wentworth swore between his teeth and walked rigidly toward the machine-gunner. He could see the blaze of the man's eyes, and he could hear the rapid beat of the priests' feet as they closed in behind him. Now his eyes could see the chamber beyond, see the poor creatures who had been tortured to bell him into this trap.

They were in a giant drum of thick glass and there was a piston that could be screwed down upon them—human grapes in a wine-press of awful torture! That was not the thing that brought Wentworth up in a quivering halt. It was the sight of the woman who stood, in chains, before the throne of Vishnu on which Kalki sat. Her eyes met his proudly, but there was suffering in the haughty lift of her head. Dear God, Nita had been captured, too!

WENTWORTH'S EYES whipped beyond her to the throne of Vishnu and, like a flick of light, his knife arm arched over and the keen blade sped through the dim light toward its target... in Kalki's breast! A dozen feet before it reached him, the knife struck something and bounded back, singing, into space. Wentworth had just time to realize that there must be a shield of bullet-proof glass before Kalki and then the overwhelming press of the attacking priests bore him to the floor.

"Don't kill him, yet," Kalki said gently. "I want him to realize to the full the thing he has accomplished. Bishop Harrington will hold his mass meeting today, within the hour, Spider, and you may give him what protection you can. Unfortunately, it won't be much. You see, Spider, you shall ride upon the cart of the Juggernaut. You and the lovely priestess here... shall ride in chains. I want you to see Bishop Harrington and all the other thousands of unbelievers perish in the flames of Vishnu!"

Wentworth was hauled up from the floor and his eyes went haggardly to Nita and read there the confirmation of what Kalki said. She had transmitted his request and his promise to Bishop Harrington! Trusting in the word of the Spider, he would assemble his congregation... to die terribly in the flames of Vishnu! And Wentworth would be chained helplessly, with Nita, to the cart of the Juggernaut, compelled to witness that destruction!

For a brief moment, Wentworth knew hope. The salt he had distributed would cause the priests to die also! Even that brief hope faded. Nita obviously had been caught with the sack of the immunity powder, since Kalki had heard her message to Bishop Harrington. It meant Kalki soon would discover the mischief that had been done to the air conditioner, if he were not already aware of it.

Wentworth felt the stiffness go out of his spine, and black despair clustered in his brain. He flung himself violently into battle, but it was a fight of desperation, without hope, and it was soon smothered. Chains loaded him down and he lay, presently, helpless, before the throne of Vishnu. Nita's eyes rested pitifully upon him, and he could give her no hope. They were doomed, and the city was doomed.

Above him, came the resonance of Kalki's awful voice. "It is time," he called. "Time to summon the faithful to the cart of the Juggernaut for the triumph of Vishnu. When this day is done, every human left alive in the city will be prostrate before Vishnu… and the churches of false gods will lie in ruins before the flames of Vishnu!"

His voice died, and rough hands seized Wentworth's chain and dragged him to his feet. As he walked like a dead man beside Nita, the chanting voices of the priests lifted high in the praises of Vishnu… Vishnu of the flames, and Kalki, the avatar of Vishnu!

CHAPTER 9
CART OF THE JUGGERNAUT

WENTWORTH WAS scarcely aware when the procession of priests entered the Temple of Vishnu itself except that a roar of voices like the drums of a hurricane beat upon him and he peered drunkenly about him. He was high on the platform at the rear of the temple and below him was a vast sea of faces, white faces with open mouths, shouting. But there was no pause. Kalki in his white robes, his massive shoulders thrown back and the red spear-thrust of his beard lifted, was marching through the lane that opened among the thousands. The golden-clad priests followed, thrusting him and Nita forward in chains.

Faces, human faces screaming at him, until the walls of the temple seemed to rock with the volume. The altar flame burned true and straight and Wentworth stared at it blankly, wondering how it could be so amid the whip and beat of this thunder…

Then the glass columns were behind him and he beheld the cart of the Juggernaut.

Thirty feet across its base, the cart lifted in a square pyramid to a peak that was an altar. Upon it poised the glistening figure of a white, winged horse… the form Kalki was supposed to take in this the tenth avatar of Vishnu. From that horse, towering a full forty feet above the pavement, flame soared straight upward into the air, a dancing, fluttering column of red and scarlet fire.

Wentworth saw these things—saw the gigantic wheels of the cart itself, the hundred ropes that would pull it and the thousands of human beings who would drag it through the streets. Nothing could stop them. Not the police, nor all the prayers of the churches, nor the power of the Spider. There were too many thousands of them, clad in the white of Kalki and chanting, singing, dancing in a kind of corybantic fury. Already, their hands were gripping the ropes of the cart.

One other thing, Wentworth saw, and for the moment, did not realize its significance… There was a water-filled pit there at the entrance of the temple and through this the worshippers of Vishnu waded, crawled, fought their way before they dashed, dripping, to seize on the ropes of the cart of the Juggernaut.

Then he was shoved up on the cart itself and chains were about his wrists, securing him to the heavy base boards. Kalki was high above him on a throne before the winged horse. The cart lurched, and there was a groan from the immense wheels. It moved forward… Far out over the heads of the straining thousands of votaries, gripping the ropes, Wentworth saw the police.

They were lined up, scores deep; mounted squadrons galloped ahead. They were clearing the street for the cart!

Wentworth found an oath deep in his throat and it came out raspingly. Yet, what else could the police do? This was a religious festival, from their viewpoint, and it is an age-old truth that whatever the body of the people wants, it will have. Apparently, the greater part of the population wanted Vishnu… and the police were, in the last analysis, public servants. They were clearing the way… and they did not know of the threat that Kalki had voiced in his temple, that every church along the path of the Juggernaut would fall in smoking ruins under the flames of Vishnu!

Something fell about Wentworth's shoulders like a cloak and a hat was slammed on his head. He looked down in wonder at the thing that fell about him. It was… Good God, they had put upon his shoulders the cloak of the Spider!

It was at that moment that Wentworth began to arouse from the torpor of despair into which he had fallen. His head came up slowly, and the old keenness flashed back into his eyes. Once more he was acutely conscious of what went on about him. He could look at Nita and see how proudly she carried her head above the scanty robes of Vishnu in which they had clothed her—could see how her violet eyes still could smile upon him.

The shouting and the chanting of the thousands who strained upon the ropes of the Juggernaut faded into a background for his thoughts and, once more, the Spider awakened to battle! But it was late, too late, his sanity told him.

"I have reserved a special treat for you, Spider," Kalki's deep voice rumbled down upon him. "You shall witness the destruction of the cathedral and the people you promised to protect. Afterward, the woman shall fling herself, an offering to Vishnu, beneath the wheels of the cart. And after that… Why, after that, I shall *permit* you to do the same! Kalki has spoken!"

Wentworth heard the words and ignored them, for his eyes were beyond Kalki upon the flame that burned straight upward from the altar that was upon the back of the winged, white horse. Straight upward… There would be a reason for that. Even the light airs that fanned the street, that swept in through the canyons of the buildings, would stir that flame somewhat… *should* stir it *but did not!* Therefore, there must be some artificial wind, some bellows beneath it that fanned the flame straight upward.

And the cart was turning… was turning into Fifth Avenue. Wentworth's eyes reached ahead, and something like a groan forced its way to his lips. There before the cathedral, a crowd of two thousand people knelt upon the steps. Their hands were upraised and, at the head of the steps, Bishop Harrington in all his regalia, carrying the sacred cross of the church, was standing!

The flame dust! Wentworth's eyes narrowed. How would Kalki spread it this time? There were no automobiles in the street to filter the awful burning stuff through the clear air of Sunday morning. Airplanes? Wentworth's eyes swung aloft, but not even a bird flung its shadow across the faultless blue arch of the heavens. There was only one conclusion. It must come from the cart of the Juggernaut itself! This pyramid would contain a hundred tons of the flame-powder and… and that straight-blown flame atop the horse could disperse it!

Once more, Wentworth twisted about to stare upward toward Kalki, toward the white altar on which the flames towered. The flames fluttered with a swifter movement; they reached higher against the burning blue sky. Yes, he was right. They were preparing. At any moment, the death-dust would begin to swirl upward into the air… and the breeze was toward the cathedral with its praying thousands! Oh, Kalki had planned damnably well!

Wentworth jerked his gaze back to the chains which bound him. They were looped under the main beam that bound together the cart of the Juggernaut. He shook his manacles, and found that whoever had secured him had done it hurriedly. The manacles were a poor fit. He had room inside them to turn his wrists. His eyes quickened. They were too tight to slip from his hands, but the chain was looped loosely under the beam. If he could free one hand, he could drag the chain free! If he could free but one hand….

Wentworth's eyes leaped ahead. A scant two blocks now to the place where the thousands prayed before the cathedral… If he was to strike, it must be now. Already, a swift plan was forming in his brain… if only he could free one hand! Wentworth's lips clamped together and there was a fierce gleam in the gray-blue eyes. He called softly to Nita.

"I am going to break free," he said. "When I do, throw yourself flat down on the platform, and against the face of the step

Nothing could stop the worshippers—not even the police, not all the

prayers of the church... not even the power of the Spider!

of the pyramid above you. You will get the maximum protection that way."

Nita turned her eyes wonderingly toward him, looked at his wrists, and she gasped at what she saw. Wentworth had set the powerful fingers of his right hand about his left and, even while he spoke, his shoulders arched with the pressure he was exerting! His face was set in a granite mold and the muscles knotted along his jaw, but there was no other indication of the fierce pain of the thing he did. But Nita knew that he was—*breaking the bones of his left hand so that it would slide free through the manacle!*

A weakness like nausea struck through Nita's breast and she twisted her own slim hands together, and set her teeth in her lip. She saw Wentworth's face quiver and a low cry was torn from her. Wentworth had a new grip upon his left hand and the sweat stood out on his temples; a grayness crept up his cheeks. The muscles of that right hand corded and....

"I am free, Nita. *Now!*"

There was the swift rattle of the chain as Wentworth whipped it from under the beam and Nita threw herself sideways, and pressed in close against the pyramid step as he had ordered. She saw the chain swing around his head like a scimitar, saw the twisted pitiful left hand hanging limply... and then Wentworth leaped past her. A confused shout lifted from the voices of the priests who stalked in their silken glory beside the cart of the Juggernaut and Wentworth went leaping up the steps of the Juggernaut, toward the winged horse, toward the throne of Kalki.

The chain whined about his head in a vicious circle, and the pain of his broken left hand was a goad. For three strides, Kalki did not see him. His eyes were peering greedily toward the cathedral steps and Wentworth saw Kalki's left hand drop to the arm of his throne, and move back along it toward a small lever set in the wood!

Wentworth knew what that meant! In a split-second, Kalki would release upon those praying thousands the flames of Vishnu, who yet were two blocks away!

WENTWORTH SHOUTED his hoarse challenge and Kalki's eyes whipped toward him. The whining chain flashed through the air and Kalki flung himself sideways, his left arm which had been so close to the lever, thrown up toward his head. Wentworth set his shoulders. He put all his strength into that snarling swing of the chain... and saw it strike Kalki's arm! The arm went limp and Kalki tumbled sideways down the steps of the pyramid, rolling, shouting curses.

For an exultant moment, Wentworth paused. A long leap and he could whirl the chain down again, upon the defenseless head of Kalki! But even as the thought flashed across his brain, the priests were swarming up to cover him with their bodies. A gun spat and the bullet whipped dangerously close to the Spider's head!

In that mad, deathly moment, Wentworth glimpsed the thing he must do. He flung the taunting, fierce laughter of the Spider into the writhing, mad faces of the priests. Then he sprang toward the white, winged horse that was the symbol of Kalki—that was the altar of Vishnu upon the Juggernaut! Once more, the chain whined through the air and it struck, and

155

looped around the neck of the poised horse! Two blocks from the cathedral....

It was a narrow margin of safety, but it must suffice. Kalki had planned to puff the death-dust high into the air and let the breeze sift it toward the praying throng before the cathedral. But suppose all the dust were released now, in this one spot? Suppose instead of being fanned into the high air, it tumbled heavily down the sides of the pyramid upon the priests!

Wentworth laughed again as the chain locked fast about the neck of the white horse. He wrapped his good arm about the chain and bowed his back in a fierce pull at the altar of Vishnu! It was his guess that the priests could not have been re-immunized after he had released the salt in the temple of Vishnu... and he knew that the devoted thousands about the Juggernaut had been! That was the purpose of that "sacred" pool before the temple, through which the thousands had waded and crawled before dashing to the ropes that pulled the cart. But the robes of the priests were dry!

Wentworth threw his whole strength into that frantic wrench upon the white horse of Kalki. He felt the altar stir, but it held fast to its base. Guns were blasting, and the mad thousands who surrounded the cart had ceased to tug at the ropes. They were shouting in fierce anger at the desecration Wentworth was committing. They began to swarm toward the cart, and over the whole street swelled the hymns from the church.

Now that the chants of the priests were stilled, that organized, rhythmic hymning of thousands of voices made itself felt.

Wentworth knew his moment of despair, wrestling with that immense weight of the horse balanced above him.

Wentworth flung himself backward once more in a final desperate effort. The white horse tilted on the platform above him. It reared on its fore-feet and the flame on its back guttered and went out. The wings spread, as wide as heaven, above Wentworth's head, and he worried at the chain. He hurled himself backward, and wrenched at it. His shoulders sawed with the effort. There were no gun-shots; there were only rising, frantic cries of despair. The stiff hind-legs of the horse lifted higher and higher. The flaring, motionless nostrils, the proud neck stooped toward Wentworth and, suddenly, the fore-feet slipped!

They slipped, and behind the white horse, Wentworth could see billowing clouds of white, flung upward by the bellows—air that had hurled the flame straight upward. A shout of triumph rose in his swelling throat. The flame-dust! *The flame-dust!* Then the horse fell....

STRAIGHT FORWARD, with the heavy dignity of an idol falling, it tipped toward Wentworth. The chain went slack in his hand, and he needed it no longer. The head plunged straight downward at the throne chair; the wings cut a flashing arc through the air. Frantically, Wentworth hurled himself flat upon one of the pyramid steps, ground his body against the face of the next above him. There was a splintering crash, and fragments of the throne chair hurtled like projectiles through the air.

Wentworth heard a thin, musical tinkling sound. Glass breaking; a thousand shards of glass were breaking. The massed shout of those grouped thousands above him soared on a rising, despairing note, and the tinkling came nearer. It deluged Wentworth—swept all about him, over him, and cascaded down over the steps toward the street.

Wentworth struggled to his feet. He was standing amid fragments of white glass. One wing tip of the white horse that had broken into shards of the glass from which it was made, was slithering down the side steps of the pyramid. That was the only whole piece that remained. And from the crest of the pyramid, the swirling white clouds of powder were still spewing. Even as Wentworth gained his feet, he heard a rising cry of agony. He stared down toward the golden-robed priests, toward the angry fanatics that were climbing toward him, and he saw their leader check. He saw the man stiffen and begin to claw at his eyes… and he saw the flames—the flames of Vishnu—burst from the man's eyes and begin their frenzied, jubilant dance over his body!

For that single instant, all men stared at that one flame-racked priest… and then they were staring no longer. Then the agony, and the flames of Vishnu were all about them. And it was a curious thing that they struck only the priests of Vishnu. They struck only the priests of the false avatar of Vishnu who called himself Kalki! In an instant, there were no more of the golden-robed men. There were only writhing things on the ground that had been human beings and now were prey for flames!

The crowds who had worshiped stared in bewilderment at this thing that was happening, gaped upward where the Spider stood bold and clear against the blue sky—with a chain swinging from his wrist, amid the wreckage of the altar before which they had worshiped.

Wentworth threw up his arms—the right arm with its dangling chain, and his left arm with the twisted and broken hand. His voice was like a trumpet, booming over the heads of the multitude.

"The Lord, Jehovah, spoke unto thee:

"Thou shalt have no other gods before me, and thou shall not kneel down and worship any graven image.

"The idolaters are destroyed! Go and sin no more!"

WHEN WENTWORTH'S voice had died out, there was no other sound at all save where the small flames of Vishnu leaped merrily over the bodies of the priests and made little crackling, snapping, frying sounds. And then, slowly the voices of the thousands before the temple began to lift, and a hymn fell softly through the street! Wentworth turned and saw the uplifted cross in the bishop's hands, but it was for another thing that he was looking.

He had gathered the chain into his hands and his keen gaze was seeking for Kalki. Kalki had not perished under the flames. Wentworth knew that, for he was looking for the man, and had not seen him.

And then, suddenly, Wentworth spotted Kalki, The man was running, staggering, around the far corner of the street—and over his shoulder, *he carried the limp form of Nita!*

A great shout welled from Wentworth's throat and he vaulted down the pyramid steps. The crowd below opened before him and, as he ran, men dropped to their knees and bumped their foreheads upon the stone pavement. But Wentworth did not see them. His eyes were on the corner around which, brief seconds before, Kalki had vanished with Nita!

Wentworth whipped around the corner and, a block away, saw Kalki fumbling with the lock of an auto door. His left arm hung limp at his side, and Nita had been dropped to the sidewalk. Wentworth flung himself into a furious sprint. His naked feet rasped on the walk, his cape billowed back from his shoulders. He sent his challenge before him, his challenge to Kalki.

The fiery head swung toward him and, for a moment the man seemed to hesitate. Then he flung himself into the car and, leaving Nita supine upon the sidewalk, wrenched the machine from the curb and sent it hurtling down the street. There was not another auto in sight and Wentworth felt defeat lay its heavy hand upon him.

Behind him, a police whistle skirled. He heard the slam of a revolver as he bent over Nita's prostrate form. Wentworth gazed down with gentle eyes upon her face. There was a slight bruise on her jaw, but otherwise she was unharmed.

Kalki had merely knocked her out… and Kalki was escaping. Wentworth jerked himself erect, whirled to see the police racing toward him, three men in police blue, with guns in their hands. They would care for Nita.

Wentworth bent to brush a curl back from Nita's forehead and saw her begin to stir, caught the flutter of her eyelids, and he straightened… and once more began to run. The guns crashed out again, but he made the corner unharmed, cast around wildly for a car, a taxi… *anything*. There was nothing. And Kalki already was out of sight!

Wentworth angled toward the distant corner, threw his body into the steady lope that covered ground so rapidly. Behind him, the beat of police feet was heavy, furious. If they held him in sight, one of their bullets might pull him down, might write *finis* forever to the Spider, but he had another, more important thing to consider. He must track down Kalki. There was no question of his returning to the temple. He must know that game was played out, whatever he planned for the future of his diabolical flames of Vishnu. No, he would have to disappear... into his own identity!

Wentworth's lips twisted into a thin smile as he ripped around the next corner seconds before the police shouts rang on the air. He had won that much then. If he could continue his race for another block... His heart was pounding heavily, and the fatigue of the long hours of struggle ate at him. There was the pain of his thigh-wound and broken hand. To hell with all that... Kalki! He must find Kalki!

HE ROUNDED the next corner and spotted a garage on a side street. There would be cars available, if he could persuade the owner to let him have one! Wentworth's lips grew grim, and he stretched his legs into a faster pace. The race was almost over. He would have to hold up for these last few yards—have to....

He ran into the entrance of the garage and there was a car being washed upon the laundry basin. There would be a key in its lock. Wentworth sprang past the man with the hose, saw the man's startled face swing toward him. Then Wentworth was behind the wheel; his hand found the key.

A shout burst out behind him as he wrenched the car violently toward the street. They would have the police on his heels within a few moments, with the license number and a description of the car. But those few minutes might give him the thing he wanted; the thing he must have. He wrenched the car to the curb before a delicatessen store and raced in, caught sight of a phone in the back room and lunged toward it.

A man yelled, threw up both hands, fled. Wentworth bent over the instrument, rapidly dialed the number of the detective agency he had employed to trace the man with the scar on his face. Dickinson was his name. Dickinson....

There was a long while of ringing, an incredible time of ringing it seemed to Wentworth and then an answer. Wentworth rapidly identified himself.

"We've been very thorough, sir," the detective office man said. "And I think we may claim success. In regards to this man Dickinson whom you wished us to trace...."

"Where is he?" Wentworth snapped.

"Well, sir, we traced him to this apartment, and there's still some clothes there, but he hadn't been there in about a week so far as we can find out, and...."

"Where, damn it!" Wentworth shouted.

The man gave him the address and Wentworth flung from the delicatessen store, leaped behind the wheel of the car whose engine he had left running. It was the slimmest chance, the only one he could muster at the present—but the man, Dickinson, had had a huge, deforming scar down the side of his jaw... and Kalki wore a fierce red beard! It was the only known way of hiding a facial scar and Dickinson had reason to hide his, since he had been convicted of operating a fraudulent religious cult!

Wentworth drove the car with the accelerator ground down to the floor. On his right wrist, the chain still clanked and rang as he whipped the car around corners, lunging always farther north, toward the apartment address the detective had given. The throbbing ache of his left hand was a dim torment which Wentworth ignored. The taste of victory was in his mouth. The taste… but not the substance!

A block away from the address that had been given him, Wentworth saw the parked coupé which Kalki had driven and a shout of triumph beat against his locked teeth. He hurled the stolen machine to the curb and flicked the key from the lock. He might have need of this car again presently! He went along the pavement at a dead run, smashed a shoulder against the glass panel of the apartment door. It shivered inward upon the tiled lobby floor and an attendant twisted a frightened face. Wentworth did not heed him, went across the lobby in long bounds and took the steps.

His breath was whistling between his teeth, but it was anger, and not the speed of his going that accelerated his heart; that made red flashes dance in his vision. That was what Wentworth told himself. He ignored the fact that he stumbled as he tried to leap the last three steps; that only a quick up-throw of his right arm saved him from crashing into the wall across the corridor.

He straightened and was plunging on toward the door of Kalki's apartment. He flung his shoulder against it, and the door whipped wide open. It was unfastened and he pitched forward to hands and knees in the corridor, twisted up his head and was staring into the fierce eyes… of Kalki himself!

KALKI'S RED beard was gone, and the fierce red hair had vanished, but there was the ugly scar of Dickinson upon his jaw! Wentworth pushed slowly to his feet in spite of the gun that jutted at him from Kalki's huge fist and there was a thin smile upon his face.

"Go ahead and shoot… Kalki," he said softly. "The police are chasing me because I stole a car. I smashed in the front door of the apartment so that they could not fail to find me here, and the boy in the lobby knows the apartment to which I came. So you see, Kalki, you cannot escape. That fracture of your left arm will damn you, and you will have a hard time now in making the police believe that your fires of Vishnu came from heaven."

Kalki smiled very slightly, and the movement of his solid lips was heavy with hatred. "You've done pretty well, Spider," he said softly. "Pretty well. So well that I shall not be content merely to shoot you. As for the police, there is more of the same treatment for them. Yes, I can see you have guessed it… the flames of Vishnu!"

As he concluded, he flung his right hand forward and dust spewed out of his sleeve, swirling white dust that billowed toward Wentworth in the doorway! Wentworth laughed. He clamped his eyes tight shut and slashed out with the chain upon his right wrist. He struck swiftly, and dodged violently to the right at the same movement, whirled and struck again.

"The flames of Vishnu!" Wentworth cried. "I have immunity

against it, Kalki, as you do! But you have lost sight of one thing, Kalki. *Your blood is salty, too!*"

Wentworth's back was against the wall and his eyes were slits. Through the swirling dust motes in the room, he could see Kalki—could see where the chain had lashed him, stripping across his left ear, tearing across the left side of his cheek. There was blood there, and there was red fury in Kalki's eyes. He lifted his revolver, and his face was twitching. Wentworth could see that the pain was eating at him and he drew back the lash of the chain to strike again… yet he hesitated.

There was power in Kalki. His whole body was fighting against the eating pain, and suddenly the flames were playing across his cheek, lapping up the blood that streamed from torn ear and cheek. They danced toward his eyes and still Kalki fought to pull up his gun, to hold it steady on the target of the Spider's spread-eagled body against the wall. A shot crashed out, but the bullet went wild. And then… and then the flames were in Kalki's eyes!

Kalki screamed out a terrible oath. He tore at his cheeks with blunt nails and the flames… spread. He whirled about, his great legs straddled as if by the very strength of his limbs he would support himself against the agony of the fire. And Kalki walked. He *ran*. And finally, he hurled himself headforemost through the air. There was the thin crash of breaking window glass and, afterward in the room, there was only the faint odor of burning hair, of singed clothing, and the swirl of the dust motes. Presently, there was a crushing thud….

WENTWORTH THREW the elbow of his arm across

165

his eyes and fumbled his way toward the door. His foot slipped and he stared down at the floor, saw there a drop of Kalki's blood that had not yet blazed. Wentworth stooped and caught up the smear and, on the door, he drew a fierce large Spider. As he drew, the flames leaped out behind the tracery of his finger, and the fire touched his flesh. He smothered it against his body and, as he ran down the hall, there burned upon the door the seal of the Spider!

He reeled frankly now in his flight and there was need for haste. He had not lied when he said the police would be hard behind him, and he knew that the boy in the lobby already would be phoning for help. The radio cars would come, as eager as hounds, and he must be away long before they came; long before... or they would be on his heels. He did not think that he could run again. He did not think that his spirit would stand up under one more frantic run from the charges of the police.

He saw the big eyes of the boy and heard his voice lift in excitement. "He's running through the lobby now. My God, he's wearing a cape. It's the Spider. The Spider, I tell you!"

Wentworth slammed out on the pavement, slipped and almost fell. The chain still clanked from his wrist, and its swinging beat against his thigh. He found the stolen car more by instinct than by vision and leaped in behind the wheel, jerked it from the curb.

Yes, the sirens were beginning again, the sirens that marked each turning of his life these days, the yelping of the police hounds, hot on the blood trail of the Spider. He had saved them—had saved the city from this last, desperate attack of

Kalki and the flame of Vishnu—but that did not matter. He was the Spider, wanted for murder. So, drag the man down, capture the quarry, shoot him on sight!

Wentworth's head reeled dizzily as he swept the heavy car around the corner and it seemed to him that he heard church music, throbbing, swelling church music, an old-fashioned hymn. He stared down, frowning with a brain that would not think, and saw the gleam of light behind a radio dial. He must, somehow, have hit the switch when he grabbed the ignition. He started to cut it off, and didn't.

How far to safety? If he could reach the garage, empty now of any car of the Spider, but equipped with clothing and weapons, he would be safe for a while... as safe as he was anywhere in the world.

The hymnal voices lifted beautifully, and ended presently while the sirens still whimpered in the distance, while Wentworth still drove with reeling senses. His left hand was an agony, and the older wound in his thigh throbbed with fever. Small injuries though; a cheap price to pay for the saving of the city, for the death of Kalki. He could heal them swiftly now if he could rest. Rest....

There was a voice over the radio, and it was a voice Wentworth knew, suddenly. Bishop Harrington. He said, "Let us pray...."

Wentworth frowned with the concentration of listening, of driving the car together. It was almost too much for his weary brain. Rest. He must have rest... What was the bishop saying?

"And, O Lord, we thank thee especially that in this hour of

our trial, thou hast sent us a man. This poor, misguided man who calls himself the Spider and fights with the weapons of his enemies, but who, nevertheless in our hour of need, was strong for righteousness and has given us the triumph over thy enemies. We thank thee especially for this Spider then, Lord. May his life be long in this world! May his joys never cease! May he have the blessings of thy hand upon him, O Lord!"

Wentworth's laughter burst forth uncontrollably, but it was with hysteria that he laughed and he throttled it. Surely, the Lord was blessing him now! But it was a transient thought, and it was humble. He had these blessings, that he had escaped alive, and that the enemies of mankind had perished once more under his hand.

He stared blindly about him, and recognized a street corner. He was near his hidden garage. He swung into the curb, and the car broke from his control and jarred across the sidewalk before it trundled to a halt against the wall. Wentworth staggered out from behind the wheel, rested for a moment against the side of the car and then ran, drunkenly, toward the alley. The sirens were still far away. He would make sanctuary.

Behind him, the radio still vibrated to the strong, rising devotion of Bishop Harrington. "And so, O Lord, from full and grateful hearts, we thank thee for this man, this strong servant of the All-Mighty. We thank thee for the Spider...."

THE SPIDER

❏ #1: The Spider Strikes	$13.95
❏ #2: The Wheel of Death	$13.95
❏ #3: Wings of the Black Death	$13.95
❏ #4: City of Flaming Shadows	$13.95
❏ #5: Empire of Doom!	$13.95
❏ #6: Citadel of Hell	$13.95
❏ #7: The Serpent of Destruction	$13.95
❏ #8: The Mad Horde	$13.95
❏ #9: Satan's Death Blast	$13.95
❏ #10: The Corpse Cargo	$13.95
❏ #11: Prince of the Red Looters	$13.95
❏ #12: Reign of the Silver Terror	$13.95
❏ #13: Builders of the Dark Empire	$13.95
❏ #14: Death's Crimson Juggernaut	$13.95
❏ #15: The Red Death Rain	$13.95
❏ #16: The City Destroyer	$13.95
❏ #17: The Pain Emperor	$13.95
❏ #18: The Flame Master	$13.95
❏ #19: Slaves of the Crime Master	$13.95
❏ #20: Reign of the Death Fiddler	$13.95
❏ #21: Hordes of the Red Butcher	$13.95
❏ #22: Dragon Lord of the Underworld	$13.95
❏ #23: Master of the Death-Madness	$13.95
❏ #24: King of the Red Killers	$13.95
❏ #25: Overlord of the Damned	$13.95
❏ #26: Death Reign of the Vampire King	$13.95
❏ #27: Emperor of the Yellow Death	$13.95
❏ #28: The Mayor of Hell	$13.95
❏ #29: Slaves of the Murder Syndicate	$13.95
❏ #30: Green Globes of Death	$13.95
❏ #31: The Cholera King	$13.95
❏ #32: Slaves of the Dragon	$13.95
❏ #33: Legions of Madness	$12.95
❏ #34: Laboratory of the Damned	$12.95
❏ #35: Satan's Sightless Legion	$12.95
❏ #36: The Coming of the Terror	$12.95
❏ #37: The Devil's Death-Dwarfs	$12.95
❏ #38: City of Dreadful Night	$12.95
❏ #39: Reign of the Snake Men	$12.95
❏ #40: Dictator of the Damned	$12.95
❏ #41: The Mill-Town Massacres	$12.95
❏ #42: Satan's Workshop	$12.95
❏ #43: Scourge of the Yellow Fangs	$12.95
❏ #44: The Devil's Pawnbroker	$12.95
❏ #45: Voyage of the Coffin Ship	$12.95
❏ #46: The Man Who Ruled in Hell	$13.95
❏ #47: Slaves of the Black Monarch	$13.95
❏ #48: Machineguns Over the White House	$13.95
❏ #49: The City That Dared Not Eat	$13.95

❏ #50: Master of the Flaming Horde	$13.95
❏ #51: Satan's Switchboard	$13.95
❏ #52: Legions of the Accursed Light	$13.95
❏ #53: The City of Lost Men	$13.95
❏ #54: The Grey Horde Creeps	$13.95
❏ #55: City of Whispering Death	$13.95
❏ #56: When Thousands Slept in Hell	$13.95
❏ #57: Satan's Shakles	$14.95
❏ #58: The Emperor From Hell	$14.95
❏ #59: The Devil's Candlesticks	$14.95
❏ #60: The City That Paid to Die	$14.95
❏ #61: The Spider at Bay	$14.95
❏ #62: Scourge of the Black Legions	$14.95
❏ #63: The Withering Death	$14.95
❏ #64: Claws of the Golden Dragon	$14.95
❏ #65: The Song of Death	$14.95
❏ #66: The Silver Death Reign	$14.95
❏ #67: Blight of the Blazing Eye	$14.95
❏ #68: King of the Fleshless Legion	$14.95
❏ #69: Rule of the Monster Men	$16.95
❏ #70: The Spider and the Slaves of Hell	$16.95
❏ ***NEW:*** #71: The Spider and the Fire God	$16.95

THE WESTERN RAIDER

❏ #1: Guns of the Damned	$13.95
❏ #2: The Hawk Rides Back from Death	$13.95
❏ #3: Gun-Call for the Lost Legion	$13.95
❏ #4: The Law of Silver Trent	$13.95
❏ #5: The Gun-Prayer of Silver Trent	$13.95
❏ #6: Silver Trent Rides Alone	$13.95

G-8 AND HIS BATTLE ACES

❏ #1: The Bat Staffel	$13.95

CAPTAIN SATAN

❏ #1: The Mask of the Damned	$13.95
❏ #2: Parole for the Dead	$13.95
❏ #3: The Dead Man Express	$13.95
❏ #4: A Ghost Rides the Dawn	$13.95
❏ #5: The Ambassador From Hell	$13.95

DR. YEN SIN

❏ #1: Mystery of the Dragon's Shadow	$12.95
❏ #2: Mystery of the Golden Skull	$12.95
❏ #3: Mystery of the Singing Mummies	$12.95

RED FINGER

❏ ***NEW:*** #1: Second-Hand Death	$24.95

www.ingramcontent.com/pod-product-compliance
Lightning Source LLC
Chambersburg PA
CBHW071216260626
47162CB00004B/1317